AN IMAGICKATION NOVEL

Hidden Magick

NANCY SMITH GIBSON

Copyright © 2021 by Nancy Smith Gibson

For information, email Cozy Cat Press at
cozycatpress@gmail.com
or visit our website at
www.cozycatpress.com

COZY CAT
P R E S S

ISBN: 978-1-952579-23-3

Printed in the United States of America

10 9 8 7 6 5 4 3 2 1

Dedication

Everything in *Hidden Magick* is fiction and came from my weird mind. Well, almost everything, that is. The 'Broken China Jewelry' project is real. The 'Women's Shelter of Central Arkansas, Inc.' is a very real service that helps abused women escape from their situation. Several years ago, as a fundraiser, they came up with the craft of making jewelry pendants out of broken dishes. They thought it would be a one-time project, but it was so popular that it continues today. Their products are sold at arts and crafts shows and shops in central Arkansas, and the funds help support safe havens for women in need of a place to find safety. This book is dedicated to them.

- NANCY GIBSON

Chapter One

■◆■

JUNIPER PENDRAGON was a sophisticated man. A world traveler. Urbane. Knowledgeable. Successful. Sought after, not only for his charm but also for his imaginative designs that graced the interiors of the mystical elite throughout his home country of America and of the world. And he knew it. It gave him satisfaction. Pride. Maybe arrogance, even.

So why? he thought, *am I so dissatisfied? Bored?* He stretched and settled his derriere more comfortably on the park bench. *I can do anything I want—go anywhere in the world with a snap of my fingers—and here I sit on a park bench, moping. The South of France? Nah! There'd be the same people doing the same things. Rio, perhaps? There's always a party going on in Rio. Or someplace exotic, someplace I've never been before, like Mongolia, or Tasmania.* Nothing stirred him enough to lift a finger to snap, point, and magick his way away.

The sunlight shone through the leaves and made dappled shadow shapes dance on his denim-clad legs. *Maybe I ought not to have . . .* The thought flickered out as quickly as it had flashed in. *I will not dwell on it. I regret nothing, not anything at all. I couldn't stand one more minute of the criticisms and arguments that started as soon as I magicked something. If they were going to reject my every idea, they should not have engaged my services.* His mind had finally reached the point where it refused to call up one single embellishment to install in the mansion that awaited his supernatural touch—the mansion where he ought to be working, using his celebrated talent to transform his client's home into a showplace. *I'll be lucky if the fighting Barringtons haven't ruined me—made me unable to design another room for the rest of my life.* He shuddered at the memory of Stan Barrington's vocal criticisms of Juniper's designs, the ones that pleased Amelia Barrington, that is. The projects that pleased Stan were the ones that Amelia despised. It was enough to drive a man—or a warlock—crazy.

He was quite sure that neither member of the fighting couple liked the way he left their formerly elegant home. *Let them figure out how to transform the place into something they like, or even back to like it was in the first place. They'll be lucky if they can find their way from the living room to the kitchen.* Juniper smiled to himself at the way he had retaliated against the last criticism of his designs, with a rearrangement of walls and rooms and style until the interior of the formerly lavish structure was unrecognizable. *What was I supposed to do when I heard for the umpteenth time, "But Juniper, that's not at all what I had in mind"? Of course it wasn't. Nothing ever was. Maybe when they have to crawl through tunnels to get from one room to another, use a climbing wall to get upstairs, fight their way through interior thunderstorms, and need a map to find the bathroom, they'll settle down and cooperate with the next designer they hire. But it wouldn't be him. It wouldn't be the famed Juniper Pendragon, aka Jumper Penn. No way.*

As he sat watching the children playing across the field and enjoying the warmth of the sunlight on his arms, pondering how he should spend his now free time, he became aware of a bundle of white fur running in his direction. *Is that a dog?* He squinted his eyes. Yes, a small, fluffy dog, running as fast as it could and headed toward him. About ten feet behind was a girl, or maybe a woman—she was too far away to tell—yelling as she pursued the pet.

"Stop, Roscoe! Stop!"

Chapter Two

■ ◈ ■

IT WAS OBVIOUS that she was an ordinary person. Anyone with an ounce of magickal ability would have used a spell or enchantment to stop the dog in its tracks so she could catch it. No need for a witch to exert energy running on such a simple task. In fact, he'd never heard of a witch running for any reason, although he thought there might be some who did it for the enjoyment. Nobody he knew personally, however.

As the dog approached Juniper, the woman called out, "Catch him! Please stop him," and Juniper whispered, "puppystop," and the pup came to him, ready to be picked up. As the woman started toward where the bench sat under the branches of a spreading live-oak tree, she caught her foot in an exposed root and went tumbling face-down in the grass.

Quickly, Juniper put the wiggling ball of fur on the bench and muttered a spell to keep it there. Hurrying to her side, he knelt on the grass beside the woman and placed his hand on her back. She was breathing heavily, obviously exhausted by the dash after the runaway dog. Her eyes were closed, but he didn't think she was unconscious, only winded. After several deep breaths she turned her head and opened her eyes. Juniper could tell they were a luminous gray, framed with long, black lashes. A wealth of black hair spread around her head, tangling in the grass.

"Are you hurt?" he asked.

She rolled over onto her back, dislodging his hand. He felt a tug of regret when that small connection between them was lost. Staring at him, she took another deep breath before answering.

"I don't think so. Did Roscoe get away?"

"No, I caught him." Juniper inclined his head toward the bench.

The woman struggled her way up onto her elbows and looked that way. "And he's staying put? Roscoe, you're a bad, bad dog!" She looked back at Juniper. "Amazing. He runs away from me, but behaves for a stranger."

"I have a way with dogs." *Not that I've ever had a dog, but I think I'd like to. If I ever settle down in one place instead of flitting around all over the world, I may get one.* He looked toward the white puff of fur on the bench, which promptly gave a small woof toward Juniper and wiggled, wanting to jump down but constrained by the enchantment that held him there. *But it would be a big dog, a man's dog, not a stuffed toy like this one.*

She sat all the way up and brushed her hands together to remove the blades of grass stuck to them. "Evidently, I don't," she said. "Or at least not that one." She ran her fingers through her hair, trying to remove pieces of grass and put the strands in some sort of order. The jet-black mane that stood out in wild disarray framed a charming face.

"Maybe you need to have a good talk with him or else get a different dog."

"He's not mine, thank heavens. He's my grandmother's dog. But he dug a hole under the fence in the backyard and ran off, so Grandmother sent me after him." She glanced at the miscreant and frowned. "You're in big trouble, Roscoe!" She started to stand up but grimaced and gave a squeak when she tried to put her feet flat on the ground.

"Here, let me help you up," Juniper said, and grasped her hands, pulling her to her feet. "Take it easy putting any weight on your feet. You might be hurt worse than you think."

At the sound of her gasp when she tried to stand firmly, he moved to her side and put his arm around her waist. "Lean on me. Let me help you to the bench. You need to sit a few minutes before you try to walk."

Carefully, they edged toward the bench. Juniper held her hands as she eased into sitting next to the squirming dog. He sat on the other side of the excited creature and put his hand on the fidgeting furball. *Calm, now. Settle down. Be still.* He sent the thought to Roscoe, who turned and looked into his eyes. Juniper could see the question, almost hear it, *You can talk to me?*

Yes, I can talk to you. Now stop all this nonsense and sit still so we humans can talk.

What if I don't want to sit still?

Then I'll keep the spell on you so you can't move! Do you want that?

Roscoe didn't answer, but stretched out with his head resting on his paws and sighed

"Which ankle is giving you a problem?" Juniper asked. "Does it hurt when you aren't trying to stand on it?"

"My left ankle. It's better now that I'm sitting down, but it still aches a bit. I think if I sit here a couple of minutes, I'll be able to walk."

Juniper thought about repairing her injuries, but to do more than simple soothing, it would take touching the injured joint, and with the way the world was going these days, he was hesitant about putting his hand on a strange young lady's person. She might slap him or yell for help. At the very least, she might accuse him of "invading her space." Furthermore, helping the attractive woman provided the diversion he'd been looking for earlier. Something to occupy his mind other than the abandoned decorating project. *So for now I'll just see how it goes,* he thought. *I don't have anything else to do but sit here with an ordinary person and talk, and it's a beautiful day for doing that.*

"I'm sorry I'm detaining you," she said. "You probably have other things to do."

"You aren't keeping me from anything," Juniper replied. "I was just sitting here enjoying the scenery." *That sounds odd, like I'm an unemployed guy with no place to go.* "Let me introduce myself. I'm Juniper Penn. I just finished a job nearby and since I'd been admiring this park for some time, I decided to take advantage of the bench and the day."

"A job near here? What do you do?"

"I'm a designer."

"A designer? Of what?"

"Rooms, mostly. Interiors."

"Like an interior decorator? People pay you to tell them how to make their house look?" Juniper thought he detected scorn in her voice.

"Not quite. They tell me how they want their house to look, and I make it look that way."

"They can't do that themselves?"

"Some people can't. Some people don't have a clue about colors or styles or where to find what they'd like to have."

"But you do?"

"Yes. I do."

She thought about that.

"Would you be comfortable telling me your name?" he asked.

"Oh, yes. Sorry. My name is Luciana Diez."

"I'm glad to meet you, Luciana Diez," he said as he shifted on the bench and extended his hand.

"And I am pleased to meet you, Juniper Penn," she said as she took it, "although not in these circumstances." She looked woefully at her ankle as she released his hand. "But I must say, I'm glad you were here to catch Roscoe." She looked down at the sleeping pup between them. "He would probably have still been running and lost for sure if you hadn't caught him."

"I'm glad I was handy."

"I guess I'd better try to get him home," she said, and made a motion to stand up, wincing as she tried to take a step.

"I think I need to help you get there," Juniper said. "You don't need to be putting all your weight on that ankle, and carrying Roscoe is going to be a problem."

Luciana frowned. "Yes, I can see that. But I hate to put you out even more."

"Don't worry about that. I assume you, or your grandmother, live close by?"

"Yes, in one of those townhouses across the street," she said, motioning toward a row of stately homes nearby.

"Why don't I carry Roscoe with one arm, and you hold onto the other one for support? We'll go slowly." He picked up the sleepy dog and sent a thought his way. *You behave, hear me? We're taking you home, and if you give me any trouble, there won't be any treats.*

Treats? There will be treats?

Not unless you're a good pup.

Juniper moved to Luciana's left side and extended his elbow. She put her arm through his, and they took slow steps toward the street that edged the park. It took much longer than he expected to make their way across the road and up the sidewalk. Coming to a stately residence fronted with a flight of steps, they stopped.

"This is it," Luciana said. "This is home. Now how am I going to get to the front door?"

Juniper studied the situation, admiring the ornate black iron that decorated the entry. *Too bad I can't magick you up there, but that would require a lot of explaining, which you wouldn't believe.* "Tell you what. I'll put Roscoe on the top step, then come back down here and carry you up."

"That would never work. Roscoe will run away again, and I'm too heavy for you to carry up these steps."

"Roscoe and I have come to an agreement," Juniper said, looking into the pup's big brown eyes. "He has agreed to be a good dog." He looked into her gray ones. "And you're not too heavy." *And it gives me an opportunity to touch your ankle and heal it.*

Luciana stayed standing at the bottom of the steps, holding onto the iron railing, as Juniper placed Roscoe in front of the door with the admonition "stay", accompanied with a point of his magick-bearing finger.

As he bent and scooped up the slight figure, he brushed his hand over her jean-clad legs. "I'll just get the grass off before you go inside," he said, although there had been none there before he put it there seconds before. His hand touched her injured ankle, and she gasped.

"Did I hurt you? I'm sorry," Juniper said, although he knew he had not.

"No, you didn't hurt me. It just tingled. Your hands must be cold."

Juniper didn't comment, just climbed the steps and put her down at the top. It was such a pleasant experience to have her in his arms, he would have held her longer, but he didn't want to push his luck.

Luciana felt in her pants pocket and withdrew a key. While she was unlocking the massive front door, Juniper picked up Roscoe, removing the spell he'd placed on the dog to make it stay where he put it. They entered a foyer that had obviously been touched by a designer, with a soaring ceiling and an ornate mirror over an antique cabinet. A display of brightly colored flowers reflected charm into the small area. From a room beyond the entrance hall, an elderly woman appeared.

"Roscoe! Oh, you've brought back my precious one," she said in a heavily accented voice.

"Ya-ya, this is Juniper Penn. He's the man who caught Roscoe. Mr. Penn, this is my abuela——my grandmother—— Sofia Diez."

"I'm pleased to meet you, Mrs. Diez," Juniper said as he gave a little bow.

"Please, you must call me Sofia. Anyone who catches my sweet Roscoe is my friend."

"Sweet, my eye," Luciana muttered.

"Luciana, do not talk ugly about Roscoe. You know he protects this house," Sofia said.

"Roscoe is your watchdog?" Juniper said. *Maybe he yelps and squeals if a stranger comes into the house. Maybe he bites ankles on command.*

"Yes," Sofia said. "He keeps witches away."

Chapter Three

■◆■

I must have heard that wrong. "Beg pardon? He keeps what away?"

"Witches. He keeps witches away from our home," the old woman said. "They're afraid of white dogs, so they will stay away."

"I've never heard that before," Juniper said.

"Si. Is true." She placed a hand over her heart as if making a pledge. "In Barcelona there were many witches. We have to watch out big way."

"Big time," Luciana said, with a slight smirk.

"Big time. We have to watch out big time. Everybody have a white dog so witches not come to their house."

"I see," Juniper said, although he didn't.

"There many witches here in America as well. Is best to be careful."

"My grandmother believes there are such people as witches," Luciana said in a low voice. "Ya-ya, people in America don't believe in witches. Mr. Penn probably doesn't."

"They should. Much trouble come from witches."

In all his life, Juniper had never heard a conversation like this one. He couldn't think of a thing to add to this strange exchange of information. He could hardly say, "Of course I believe in witches. I am one," so he remained silent.

He was saved by the entry of another woman who could have been a twin to Luciana, except a few years older and more polished. They had the same olive skin and black hair, but where the woman he'd helped home was dressed in worn jeans and a frayed khaki jacket and wore no makeup, this new person was groomed and dressed in high style. The suit she wore was probably from a top designer and fit like a glove, emphasizing every curve of her body. The high collar gave way to a deep V neck that pulled Juniper's gaze to the bulging globes that were barely contained by the fabric covering them. It was with effort that Juniper pulled his scrutiny back to her face. The slight widening of her smile indicated that she noticed and approved of his interest.

"There are no such things as witches, Ya-ya," the stranger said. "That's an old-wives tale."

"Don't upset her, Valentina. Let her believe what she wants to believe. It does no harm," Luciana said, frowning.

"And who, pray tell, is this?" Ignoring Luciana, the newcomer walked across the foyer to stand in front of Juniper.

"This is Juniper Penn. He helped catch Roscoe, who ran off yet again. Juniper, this is my sister, Valentina."

"I'm so pleased to meet you, Mr. Penn," Valentina said as she extended her hand toward him, smiling. "Grandmother would be lost without her precious dog to protect her from witches."

"I'm glad I could be of service," Juniper said, taking the offered hand. Her smooth, cool fingers lingered in his after he loosened his grip, and they trailed across his palm as she withdrew. Signaling her interest? He wondered. As he looked

into her deep brown eyes, her smile widened slightly, and he was sure he was right.

"Come, come," Grandmother Diez said, waving her hands. "We must go sit. Valentina, you will pour us some wine. We will celebrate Roscoe's rescue by this brave young man." She motioned them toward a room opening off the entrance hall.

"It was hardly brave, Abuela, to catch Roscoe as he ran by," Luciana said in a grouchy tone.

"Now, now. Just because you weren't the one to grab Ya-ya's pet and get the praise, don't begrudge Mr. Penn," Valentina said as she slipped her hand around Juniper's arm and gently guided him into the living room beside her.

"I wasn't, I . . ." Luciana shook her head, abandoning the argument.

"Luciana did her part in catching Roscoe." Juniper felt he had to come to her defense. "She chased him my way so I could nab him."

Valentina abandoned the subject. "Sit here, Mr. Penn," she said, offering him a seat. "We often have an aperitif at this time —family time, so to speak. I imagine our parents will be home shortly. They'll want to thank you as well, I'm sure, for your part in the rescue."

She walked over to a tall, magnificently carved cabinet and threw open the doors to reveal bottles of every imaginable kind of liquor, along with sparkling crystal glasses. Opening a similar door on the lower half revealed a wine rack behind a glass panel. "Ya-ya, what shall I pour for you?"

"You should serve our guest first, Tina," she replied, and turned her hand toward Juniper.

"I'll have whatever you're having, Mrs. Diez."

The elderly lady beamed. "I would like a glass of red wine, Tina, and one for Mr. Penn."

"Is that to your taste, Mr. Penn?" Valentina asked.

"It is," he answered. "And please call me Juniper." He noticed that Valentina didn't ask her sister what she wanted. Either Luciana drank the same thing each time, or . . . Surely Valentina doesn't just ignore her sister.

"Juniper. That is an unusual name," Mrs. Diez said. "Is there a story behind it?"

"In a way. It is custom in my mother's family to bestow names of a tree or flower on the hapless new-born while they're too young to protest. My mother's name is Mimosa, although everyone calls her Mimi, and my sister is Ziniyah. I'm lucky I'm not named Rose."

Everyone was laughing when a strange deep voice entered the conversation.

"Are we missing a party?" the newcomer asked.

Chapter Four

■ ◆ ■

A DISTINGUISHED COUPLE stood at the entrance. The man was of moderate height, olive skinned as his mother and daughters, with graying hair and mustache. He was tastefully dressed in a business suit. The woman by his side was obviously also of Spanish descent, attractive, well-dressed, and had a questioning look on her face.

"Ah, son, welcome home. We are celebrating the rescue of my darling Roscoe," Sofia said.

The man smiled knowingly. "Ran off again, did he?" he advanced toward Juniper. "And since you're the only person who's not a member of my family, you must be the rescuer," he said as he extended his hand. "Hugo Diez. Welcome to my home." His voice held a hint of the accent that was so strong in his mother's speech.

"Juniper Penn. Thank you, Mr. Diez."

Diez leaned in closer as he shook Juniper's hand. "Glad it was you to get the little beast, and I didn't have to go looking for him again." He released the handclasp and turned to the rest of the group.

Minutes later, greetings exchanged and drinks served, Hugo Diez took the seat next to Juniper. "How did you happen upon my mother's pet, Mr. Penn?"

"Juniper, please. I was sitting in the park, and Luciana was chasing Roscoe, who ran up to me. I just grabbed him before he could take off again."

"And how did you come to be sitting in the park?" Juniper knew this was a polite way of asking, "don't you have a job?"

Might as well give him something to chew on. "I had abandoned a job I was working on and went to the park to regain my composure. I was thinking calming thoughts when I heard Luciana calling "stop him" and saw Roscoe running my way."

Eyebrows raised, Hugo Diez stared at Juniper a moment before saying, "Abandoned your job?"

Luciana entered the conversation from across the room where she was seated next to her mother. "He's a decorator, Papa. An interior decorator. He helps people make their homes beautiful, like you see in magazines."

"Is that right?" Hugo asked.

"In a way," Juniper replied. "Sometimes. These days I primarily design commercial spaces. Shops, eating establishments, public areas. Sometimes I find time to accommodate private parties who want something special in their homes." He looked to where Luciana was staring at him, her mouth open. "Unfortunately, the couple I was working with couldn't agree on what their home should look like. I'd had enough of their bickering and left." He swirled the wine in his glass. "As I said, I was regaining a sense of peace, which is important to me."

"Ah," Hugo Diez exclaimed. "That I understand. Peace is important to a man if he hopes to accomplish his goals. Indeed, it is even important to me in my line of work, although others might not understand that."

"And what line of work is that, if I may ask?"

"Imports," Hugo Diez said. "In the old country I would have said exports. Then the company grew to the point my brother and I decided to have offices and warehouses here in America as well as in Spain. I moved my family to this new country to facilitate the distribution and the finding of new customers, while my brother remains in Barcelona and manages that side of the business."

"Interesting," Juniper said. "And what do you import?"

"Many things," Hugo said. "And the list grows rapidly. We import olive oil and wine, as you might expect, along with much you might not think of. Fabrics and fiber products, for example, and cork."

"Cork for the wine bottles?" Juniper asked.

Hugo chuckled. "Yes, we sell to several manufacturers of corks for bottles, but also cork for flooring and other things."

"Interesting," Juniper said. "I might have used your product and not known it."

"What are you working on now?" Valentina asked.

"My brother-in-law is an architect, and presently I'm working with him on a project for the gentrification of an old section of downtown. When the rebuilding is further along, I'll be doing more on the individual shops. At this point, it's more plan a bit, then wait for the permits and workmen. That's why I was working on a private residence."

"Who's your brother-in-law?" Hugo asked. "Is he someone I might have heard of?"

"Paul Keaton. He designs homes and smaller commercial spaces."

"Have you done anything that we may be familiar with?" Valentina asked.

"Possibly," Juniper replied. "Although I've done many offices I feel sure you haven't visited. Attorneys and such. Do you know of the shopping center The Place in the Woods? You might be familiar with it."

"I've heard of it," Mrs. Diez said. "On the west side, isn't it?"

"Yes, it is."

"Although," Hugo Diez interjected, "Valentina may have seen some of the law offices. She's an attorney," he said proudly.

"A paralegal, Papa. Not a lawyer quite yet," she said, smiling toward the men.

"Almost a lawyer. She will take the test soon, and then will be a lawyer, instead of this para . . ."

"Paralegal," Valentina prompted. "I'm working in the field to gain experience as I study."

"Then she will become part of the family business," Hugo said. "The attorney for our company. She's studying those laws that pertain to import and export." He beamed at his daughter.

"And you?" Juniper turned toward Luciana. "Will you become part of the family's firm someday?"

He heard Valentina's snort as Hugo spoke. "Not likely. Not bloody likely." Looking toward Luciana, he felt, rather than heard, a sigh and saw her press her lips firmly together, as if holding in her words.

Juniper didn't like to be present during awkward moments in the lives of strangers. It sounded like something was awry, something potentially embarrassing, and he didn't want to be involved. "Would you look at that," he said, glancing at the gold watch on his wrist that hadn't been there a minute before. "I didn't realize how late it's getting. I have a business appointment I need to be at shortly." He placed his wine glass carefully on the table at his side and stood. That's when he discovered that he was firmly anchored to the floor by Roscoe, who was spread across Juniper's feet, sleeping soundly.

"Oh, how sweet," Sofia gushed. "My Roscoe has attached himself to our guest. That is a good sign. Roscoe knows those things," she said. "He is a good judge of people." She smiled up at Juniper. "He knows you are a good person."

Like a witch? Juniper thought. He carefully moved his feet from under the dog, who opened one eye, then went back to sleep. "Thank you for your hospitality," he said to Hugo Diez, who'd risen and extended his hand. "I'm glad to have been of service, and to have met your family, but I must be going."

He'd taken only one step toward the foyer when Valentina slipped her arm through his. "Let me see you to the door," she said. He could have bet money on the fact she would do so. *And I didn't even have to do any magick,* he thought.

If there was one thing Juniper considered himself an expert in——besides magickal design——it was women. It was about the time he started paying attention to girls, which was in nursery school, that they started paying attention to him. He soon discovered that it didn't take any magick at all for females, from kindergarten tots to grandmothers, to coddle and compliment him, going out of their way to provide him with whatever they thought he might want or need. Little girls shared their cookies with him, while old ladies patted his cheek and said things like, "I wish I was fifty years younger." Juniper was used to reading messages from women, both stated and unstated. He had a lot of practice in both.

He could hardly miss the signal the lovely lawyer-to-be gave as they walked toward the exit. She held his arm firmly against the side of her voluptuousness, and the coy smile she sent his way assured him that he could see and touch more if he played his cards right. With her other hand, she reached toward a dish on the console in the foyer and plucked a business card. Tucking it in his shirt pocket, she said, "Here's my phone number at work. Call me sometime. Perhaps we can . . .," she paused as she opened the front door. She released his arm and ran her fingers slowly from bicep to wrist. "Meet for a drink," she said, looking into his eyes as if inviting him to read more in their brown depths. "Or something."

His answer was slowly forming in his brain as he weighed the thought of the brief pleasure he might enjoy with this obviously narcissistic and self-absorbed but beautiful woman with the trouble an affair with an ordinary woman could cause when another voice spoke.

"Mr. Penn," Luciana said, "I just wanted to say thank you for helping me home when I couldn't walk, and for helping me with Roscoe."

She stood in sharp contrast to her sister, although Juniper could see that they favored each other enough to almost be twins. For a moment he wondered if they were, in fact, the product of one egg that had split, but no one would ever confuse them with each other. One was as polished as a fashion model, sleek and smooth in dress and composure, while the other was tousled and disheveled, with grass stains on the knees of her worn jeans, a tear in the old khaki shirt she wore as a jacket, her hair going in all directions, and there, on her elbow, and again in her hair, were blades of grass he had missed when he had brushed her off.

Juniper frowned. *How could I think even for a moment that they might be twins? Valentina is an adult, while Luciana is still a schoolgirl, still a teenager, not yet grown.*

"I was happy to help you, Luciana. I'm just glad I was handy when Roscoe ran by." He smiled at her, briefly, until Valentina put her hand on his arm and turned him once more toward the open doorway, gently easing him out.

"I'll be looking forward to hearing from you," she said, as she closed the door behind him.

Of course you are, he thought.

Chapter Five

■◆■

"It's time for the shops to take on personalities," Juniper said, as he stood, arms folded, surveying from across the street.

"Before they take on personalities, it's time to be sure this is what you and the clients have in mind," Paul answered, "Before we get much further. Changes would be easy now, not so much later."

"That's what today is for, isn't it? To be sure both inside and out is what everyone wants. Of course, corrections could be made later, but . . ." Juniper stopped speaking.

"But anything made with bricks and mortar, not . . ." Paul looked around to see that nobody was standing nearby, "magicked, should be the way we want it by this point. The contractor is wanting to sign off, if we're happy."

"That's all we need, the brick and mortar, the electrical and plumbing, everything essential, to be firmly established and to code. That's where you come in." Juniper said. "verifying that part. Then my part starts." He grinned. "That's when the fun begins."

"I'm looking forward to seeing what you're going to do," Paul said. "I'm not used to all this magick stuff yet, and I have to tell you, it blows me away to see it."

"You brought everything up to today's standards by conventional methods," Juniper said. "Everything is like new and completely functional. Now I'm going to make it look like we're in . . . somewhere . . . London, maybe, or Belfast, a hundred years ago."

"That will be interesting. Can I watch?"

"I wouldn't mind, but I'll need to do it when nobody is around to see. People will see it this way," he motioned up and down the block of shops, "and the next time they drive or walk by, it'll be changed, and they'll think 'I wonder when they did that? It wasn't that way the other day.' And I'll do it a little bit at a time. I can get the atmosphere I want better that way." He took a step toward the street. "Show me which shop is which."

"Madame Aragon's shop is staying just as it was, of course," Paul said as they crossed the street in front of the couturier's business. "It was the only shop on the block that remained, and it's already perfect. We didn't touch it in any way. Down that way to the right will be the tea shop.

"What's next?"

"The bookstore," Paul pointed. "The owners of this block, the Pellegrinos, tell me a jewelry maker is inquiring, and others as well."

"Sounds like they'll have plenty of renters," Juniper said.

"Yeah. I wouldn't have thought there would be so many er . . . special people in this city."

"Well, yes, it would surprise you, I guess. I think there's a florist in town, but he's well established where he's located. He probably wouldn't want to move."

"They mentioned one shop that might give you some problems with the interior design," Paul said.

"The cobbler?"

"Yes, the shoemaker. I understand he's very, uh, different, and needs his home and his workshop to be quite . . . um . . . special."

Juniper grimaced. "I've been chewing on that ever since they told me. Trolls are notoriously hard to get along with."

"He's a troll?" Paul's eyebrows raised. "I thought trolls were only in fairy tales."

"Oh no, they're real all right. Rare but real. They're some kin to leprechauns, I think."

Paul's eyes widened. "Are you saying leprechauns are real too?"

"These days we say 'little person', but not all little people are leprechauns or trolls. In fact, very few little people have mystical blood." Juniper shook his head. "Trolls prefer to live underground, but I don't think there's any way I can pull that off."

"If they're that antisocial I wouldn't think he'd even want to have a business here in town."

"I wouldn't either, but how else is a cobbler going to sell handmade shoes, even magick shoes? From a cave somewhere?" Juniper asked.

"You have a point," Paul agreed.

"Besides, this troll, or little person, has a wife who's not a troll, I understand. She's insisting they live in town. She's tired of country life."

"I guess you'll be working to please the wife as well as the shoemaker," Paul said.

"Did you have any trouble with the city about the trees?" Juniper asked.

"Code compliance started to say something, but there were still two trees living from when they were last planted, about twenty years ago, and you can see the places where the others used to be. That set the precedent for there being trees here." Paul shook his head. "How those two held on all this time when the others all died is something else."

"They'll hold on now. My mother knows a hedge witch who was all too happy to come communicate with them. She was in charge of planting the new ones. The spots that were already here, where there had been trees in the past, she dug deeper, put new dirt and nutrients in them. She comes by and talks to them. Gives them encouragement. Tells them what's going on. Mimi helped her with the planting."

Paul sighed. "I marvel at all I've learned the last couple of years. Ever since I married into your family, it's just one new thing after another. I'd have thought someone who talked about getting a hedge witch who talks to trees was crazy, and now I've had one working on the garden at my house, as well as here."

"Probably the same woman who did this." Juniper studied the store fronts up and down the block, then turned to his companion. "You happy with it? Everything hunky-dory with the city? All the utilities working as they should?"

"I'm happy," Paul replied. "Every remodel should be so easy."

"That would be true if witches were involved in every step." Then he thought about the couple whose house design he had abandoned. "Witches who get along, that is.

"I've got to be going," he said. "I have a date."

Chapter Six

■ ◆ ■

JUNIPER EASED HIS JAG from one lane of traffic to another as he pulled up to a stoplight. He could have blinked his eyes and been at his destination without the hassle of cross-town congestion, but he found that the time spent driving offered an opportunity for thinking—for introspection or planning. He'd spent his lifetime hopping from one event to another, just like he did women, but as he approached thirty, he was beginning to slow down and think before he jumped, as the old axiom advised.

It had been three weeks—no, more like four—since he'd pulled out the business card Valentina had slipped in his pocket, knowing that he would eventually give in to curiosity or enticement and contact her. It had only taken a couple of days for him to succumb and call her. Why he asked her out was one of the things he thought about as he sat, caught in the post rush-hour drive.

She's beautiful, but so are a lot of women I meet. And she's an ordinary. Maybe that was the attraction, that she was an ordinary woman, not a witch or a witch-in-training. He had to admit that he was tired of the type woman he was used to dating. The Bambis and Peaches and Kikis of the mystical community were plentiful. Beautiful and flashy and all too eager to accompany an accomplished warlock from party to party, from yacht to luxury hotel, from Europe to Fiji, wherever the action was. They benefited from the world-wide travel, from the famous people they met, and often from the expensive baubles bestowed upon them when they gushed about the diamonds in a shop window or the latest model car in the showroom.

Juniper thought about his sister. Ziniyah's first marriage was to a flashy warlock who died trying to make a car fly. *The sight of that wreck sure cured any thoughts I might have had of trying anything like that. The marriage wasn't all bad, though. She got a daughter out of it.* He smiled as he thought of precocious Daisy, light of her uncle's life. *Marriage might not be so bad if I could have a daughter like Daisy. And Zin got a winner when she married Paul Keaton, with a bonus in his son, Jinky. But she thought Paul was ordinary when they started dating. It wasn't until later that she learned there was a magickal side to Paul and his son.*

Maybe that's what I'm doing, he thought. *Maybe I'm seeing if it would work for me, finding an ordinary to love, to fit into my life.*

But it's not going to be this one. Valentina was already beginning to wear on his nerves. She was as mercenary as any of the chick-witches he'd dated. *This is probably going to be the last of her. I need to let her down after dinner—politely if possible. After all, I'm a gentleman, and I want to continue to feel good about myself.*

As he approached the Diez home, Juniper thought about Valentina's admiration of expensive cars. *She likes this Jag,* he thought. He grinned as an idea came to mind. The car he pulled to the curb had suddenly become a five-year-old Ford. *I wonder what she'll say about this.*

What she'd said was, "What are you doing driving this wreck? Where's your Jaguar?"

"It's in the shop. It needed repairs."

"When do you get it back?"

"I'm thinking about not getting it back. It's too expensive to keep repaired and to drive. I may just keep this one. It serves the purpose of getting me around." He glanced to the side to see how Valentina was taking it.

"That's the wrong thing to do," she explained earnestly. "People judge you by what you drive. You want everyone to think you're a successful designer, so you need to drive an automobile that advertises that. They'll think you're a loser driving this car."

And you don't want to be seen dating a loser, do you, Valentina?

Juniper thought about changing the dinner plans, but he had reservations, and there was no sense punishing himself. He enjoyed dining at the Top of the Town. The chef was top-rate and the view couldn't be beat. Valentina had been impressed when he'd told her where they were dining this evening. Just the opposite of their second date, when he'd taken her to a blues bar and grill where an awesome group had been playing, and the hamburgers were fat and dripping. No, she hadn't liked that place at all, and she'd let Juniper know that it was far beneath her standards.

They ascended the twenty floors to the top of the upscale hotel. A bill slipped into the waiter's hand got them a table by the windows overlooking the twinkling lights of the city, but Valentina was more interested in the other people in the restaurant.

"That gray-haired man over there," she said, looking around the room, "that's the senator from this district. He's thinking about running for president. I wonder if that's his wife with him."

"Do you want a cocktail or a glass of wine?" Juniper asked, then relayed the order to the waiter patiently standing by. He ignored her running commentary about the people in the room.

"And the man behind you was in our office the other day. He's very wealthy. He has millions, if not billions." Her eyes were wide as she related this fact. It didn't impress Juniper, who'd met many millionaires and several billionaires, both mystical and ordinary. His own father was one, in fact, but he wasn't going to be letting that information slip. He'd never be rid of her then.

It took pulling her back from scanning the room several times before she could decide on what she wanted to eat. Juniper thought she'd probably order the most expensive item offered, and it was only later that he realized that her menu, as was the custom in many elegant restaurants, had no prices on it. She was choosing blind, so to speak.

"So, what are you doing at work these days?" he asked, truly interested in her job, not just starting a conversation. What people did for a living and why they did it was always of interest to him.

"Oh, boring stuff. Double-checking contracts. Researching. I hate researching."

"What will you be doing for the family business once you pass the bar and go to work there?"

She gave a self-conscious laugh and picked up a spoon, turning it over to look at her reflection in the back. "The same thing. Except I'll get to write the contracts, instead of checking ones that other people write."

"I guess it's valuable, then, to be reading the ones other lawyers have written," Juniper commented.

"I guess." She shrugged and tossed the spoon back onto the

table. She adjusted the already low neckline of her dress even lower and smiled toward him. "And what are you designing presently?"

"Today," Juniper said, leaning back in his chair, "I worked with a cantankerous shoemaker, designing his shop." He didn't say that the shoemaker was a troll, and that trolls were notorious for being bad tempered, and that he was trying to make the displays look dark, expensive, and secretive while putting spotlights on the shoes at the same time. That part was hard to explain.

"Shoemaker? Like handmade, custom shoes?"

"Yes, like that. Made to order shoes, guaranteed to fit. Expensive custom shoes and boots."

"Do you suppose he'd give me a good discount? Since you're designing his shop?"

"I doubt it," Juniper replied. "If you ask, he'll probably double the price."

"Hmmm." She frowned as she digested that strange bit of information. "What other shops are you designing?"

"A bookstore was the first to go in. We did the front today. It . . ." He started to tell her that it had a hewn stone threshold to enter, and the dark green façade looked like it had last been painted when Charles Dickens was writing novels. He stopped himself. She wouldn't understand the appeal.

"What else?"

"A tea shop, with a couple of tables and chairs on the front patio. People can sit there and sip their coffee or tea and watch the birds building a nest in the tree a few steps away."

"Eww. That sounds nasty. You might get bird poop or feathers or something in your cup." She made a face.

By the time the meal was over, Juniper hadn't enjoyed the food nearly as much as he'd anticipated. He was thinking about how to go about breaking up with this avaricious woman, *Not here in public. Maybe in the car when I take her home,* when she placed her hand on top of his.

"You know, they say the rooms in this hotel are as luxurious as any hotel in New York City. If you wanted to check it out, spend the night in one, I wouldn't object." She leaned forward, giving him a view of what he could expect to see more of if he accepted her suggestion.

How do I get myself out of this? Start coughing? Feign a heart-attack? Or be rude but honest and say "I'm not interested in spending the night with you, Valentina. I'm not even interested in having sex with you and not spending the night. I'm not interested in seeing you again.

He opened his mouth, not knowing what would come spilling out, when the delicate chime of a cell-phone flowed over the table, and Valentina reached for the evening bag by her napkin. "Sorry," she said. "I forgot to turn it off."

She glanced at the screen to see who was calling, then answered rudely, "I'm busy, Luciana. What do you want? . . . Jail? Luce, what are you doing in jail?" she demanded.

Chapter Seven

■ ◆ ■

AS JUNIPER PULLED AWAY from the valet parking stand, he couldn't help but think about the divine intervention that had gotten him out of a difficult situation. That had to be it. Divine intervention. The subject of spending a night of passion with Valentina was off the table now that an emergency had presented itself, and he was spared the ordeal of telling her that it wasn't going to happen. Luciana's trouble erased his own.

"I knew . . . I just knew that she'd get herself in trouble one of these days. Jail! I'm so embarrassed that my sister, my very own sister, is in jail."

"Did she say what for?" Juniper asked.

"No. She just asked me to come to the jail. This has been building for a long time. A long, long time. Since we were children."

"She's been in trouble before this?"

"It's the people she hangs out with, her acquaintances. The worst kind. Even when she was a kid—it started way back then. The children she chose to play with—rag-tag kids from bad families—even when she was young, and when she reached her teens it was worse. Papa didn't want them coming around our house."

He didn't know what to say to that, so he remained quiet and let her rant about her sister's behavior.

"When she was fifteen, she moved a girl into her room. We didn't even know she was there for a week. Luce kept her hidden. When Papa found out, he was furious. 'She might steal from us,' he told Luce. 'She has to go.' And Luciana begged to let her stay, but he wouldn't back down.

"Anybody I ever saw her with looked like a juvenile delinquent—every one of them. They had old, shabby clothes, and some of them were even dirty. It's a wonder she didn't get fleas or lice or something." She lapsed into brief silence.

After a few minutes, Valentina started speaking again. "She used to steal food from the kitchen. She would raid the refrigerator and the pantry. Cook could never count on the groceries being there when she got ready to prepare a meal."

"She . . . uh . . . Luciana ate that much? She's so slim, it doesn't look like she eats extra." Juniper was puzzled.

"Oh, she didn't eat it herself. She gave it away."

"Gave it away? To who?"

"Who knows? Strangers. People she met in the park. Anyone." After a moment she said. "And Mama could never keep her clothed. She gave her clothes away too."

"Clothes? She gave her clothes away?"

"Yes. Mama would ask her, 'Luciana, didn't you like the sweater I bought you? It was from a designer shop. It cost a lot of money.' and Luce would answer, 'Oh, yes, Mama. It was pretty. I liked it a lot.' But she gave it away." She sniffed, whether in sadness or in distain, Juniper couldn't tell. "When Mama bought me something, I kept it. I wore it. I value nice things, I don't give them away."

"Hmm," was all he could say. *I wonder what the story is behind all this? She must have had a reason. Or else mental problems of some sort.*

"One time, Mama bought her a dress—a particularly expensive dress—and she hadn't seen Luce wear it, so she told her to go put it on, so she could see how it fit, and you know what Luce said?"

"That she had given it away?"

"Yes. Exactly. That she had given it away. And Mama asked her why she'd done that, and she said, 'Because Patty liked it, and she needed a dress.' Mama said, 'Then let Patty's mother buy her a dress. I paid a lot of money for it, and it was for you, not for Patty.'

"It's been that way all her life. I swear, if we didn't look so much alike, I'd think she was adopted. She doesn't fit into our family at all."

Valentina gazed out the window at the passing scene. After a few minutes, she said, "Papa used an old saying when he talked to Luce. If you lay down with dogs, you'll get up with fleas. I'm afraid Luce has been associating with riff-raff so long it has rubbed off on her. I hope that whatever she's gotten herself into, Papa can get her out of it."

It was late in the evening, and there were plenty of parking places near the main entrance to the police station. Valentina took his arm to enter the big door that opened into what looked like a reception area. There were chairs, empty for the most part, lining the wall, and a long counter topped with a glass barrier. An officer in uniform stood behind the partition, shuffling papers. He didn't even glance at them as they entered.

When the woman seated in one of the chairs stood, picked up a briefcase and started toward them. Juniper thought at first it must be Luciana's attorney. Dressed in a business-like skirt and matching jacket, her hair was pulled back in a severe bun, and she was wearing large, black-framed glasses.

"Thanks for coming, Val. I'm sorry I had to interrupt your evening, Mr. Penn."

Luciana? This no-nonsense executive is the waif who was chasing a dog in the park and almost fell into my arms?

"I thought you were in jail," Valentina said.

"Why would you think that?"

"You said . . ."

"I said that I was at the jail, not in it. Don't you ever listen to what I say?"

Valentina looked sulky at the rebuke.

"Never mind. Let's go. This has been a long, tiring, hell of a day, and then my car gave out on me." Luciana looked at Juniper. "I take it you're driving? Thank you for rescuing me once again. I wasn't looking forward to trying to get a taxi or an Uber to come to the jail for a fare. They're distrustful about such things."

Juniper was fascinated by the turn of events. Nothing like a trip to the local lock-up to spice up an evening. *There must be an intriguing story behind all this,* he thought, and he was interested in hearing it. "No problem. No problem at all. Let's go."

"If you'd buy a decent car, you wouldn't have these problems," Valentina said, trotting along behind the striding Luciana, struggling to keep up despite her high heels. Juniper took her by the arm before she toppled over.

"A decent car wouldn't last an hour in my neighborhood," Luciana said. "Only junkers stand a chance of remaining intact. Last week, somebody stole the radio out of the receptionist's car while she was at work. My vehicle's so old they don't touch it." She looked chagrinned. "It just breaks down a lot."

They reached his car, which was still the one he was sure Luciana, as well as Valentina, would class as a junker. He was glad it wasn't the Jaguar he'd started out with. Although he could have protected it with a spell and left it with the assurance it would still be intact when he returned, he might have felt a bit embarrassed by having such a showy automobile in this moment. Valentina stood by the front passenger door, waiting for Juniper to open it. He punched the remote, and as soon as Luciana heard the corresponding click, she opened the back door for herself and climbed in. Valentina held his arm as he opened the front door for her and she maneuvered her long legs inside.

When they pulled away from the jail, he asked, "Is your car on the street somewhere? Do we need to make arrangements for it?"

"I've already taken care of it. I've got a place—Gary's Garage—that works with me. He came and towed it. Again. He'll call me when he gets it fixed."

"Nice to have someone you can depend on like that," Juniper said.

"I helped his family one time," Luciana replied. "His daughter . . ." Her voice trailed to a stop. "He keeps me going," she finally said.

"What in heaven's name were you doing at the jail?" Valentina asked.

"Making sure a man stays locked up," Luciana replied.

Juniper glanced into the rear-view mirror, trying to catch a glimpse of her face. "What did . . ." he trailed off. This wasn't any of his business, but he was curious anyway.

"Luce?" Valentina turned toward her sister. "Did someone hurt you? What did he do to you?"

Chapter Eight

■◆■

"Not to me—to his wife."

"Oh." Valentina turned back to face forward. "And you got involved."

"It's my job, Val. It's my job to help her. And even if it weren't, I would do it anyway." Luciana took a deep, shuddering breath. "If not me, who? If not for me, or someone like me, a woman would be dead tonight."

In the mirror, Juniper saw her shake her head, then lean it back against the seat, closing her eyes.

He pulled up to the curb in front of the Diez townhouse. "You need to get some sleep. You look exhausted," he said.

"Oh," Luciana said, sitting up straight. "I didn't think . . . I don't live here. I can't go in. My parents . . . I'm sorry I wasn't thinking."

"You don't live here?" Juniper asked.

"No. I was just here the other day, the day we met, visiting my grandmother. Then her dog ran away, and I went after it, and . . ." She trailed off.

Valentina spoke up. "She's trying to say that she wouldn't have been here if Roscoe hadn't run off and you caught him and helped her home. When she comes to see Ya-ya, she always leaves before our parents get home. Otherwise, she'll get another lecture from Papa. The other day she got caught before she could get away."

"Listen, little sister . . ." Luciana said.

"Little sister?" Juniper looked from one woman to the other.

"Yes." Luciana sighed. "I'm the oldest. The one who ought to know better. The one who ought to be the responsible sister. The one who brings trouble to the family." She put her hand over her eyes. "I might as well go in and get it over with." She reached for the door handle.

"Wait," Juniper said. "Stay where you are. Let me walk Valentina to the door, and then I'll take you home."

"I don't want to put you to all that trouble," Luciana said, trying to open the car door. "I've already interrupted your date. I'm sorry for that."

I'm not, Juniper thought. *You interrupted it at the perfect time.*

"I said," he said firmly. "Stay where you are and I'll take you home." This time he pointed his finger, and unseen magic kept the door closed.

Valentina clung to his arm as they climbed the steps to the elegant front door. "I'm so sorry our evening was interrupted," she said, placing her hands on his chest. "We'll have to continue another time." Her smile left little doubt that she was referring to a night in a luxurious hotel room.

Juniper——as do all people——had certain life rules. Beliefs that affected his actions. Such as not telling a lie. Not that he never did so, but his parents had instilled in him at an early age an important tenet of witchcraft——the importance of doing no harm, with or without using magick. When he was a young boy, a simple lie had led to repercussions and someone had been harmed. Karma had done what karma does, paid back threefold. So now, in Juniper's mind, a lie was lumped in with doing harm. If he could get by without telling one, he did. He would avoid. He would leave an erroneous impression. But that was as far as he would go.

Now Juniper was facing a woman who fully intended to take him to bed. He fully intended not to go. *Should I tell her there won't be a next time? Have a scene right here on the front steps of her parents' home? In front of her sister?*

"And on our next date, be sure to drive your Jaguar. I don't want to ride in——" She glanced at the car awaiting him.

He sighed and looked away from her. *Tell her, boy,* he told himself. *Tell her no more dates. No more Jag. No more anything. Get it over with.* "Uh, Valentina . . ."

"Why are you looking that way?" Valentina was on alert. She knew something was wrong. "Oh, I've got it now. You've lost the Jag. It's gone. It's been repossessed, hasn't it? You've been wining and dining me, trying to make a good impression, but you couldn't keep up the payments and they took it back.

"That's why you didn't act excited over getting a hotel room tonight. They run five hundred dollars a night at that place, and you couldn't afford it. If Luciana hadn't called when she did, you'd have weaseled out of spending the night with me, wouldn't you?"

Juniper remained quiet, just looking into her eyes. She was taking care of the breakup without any help from him. *That's Karma for you. Live a good life and problems take care of themselves.*

"Well, that's it. If you can't run with the big dogs, don't come around me. I don't do poor. I don't do cheap. I don't date fakes."

Of course you don't.

She went in and slammed the door behind her.

Juniper smiled as he returned to the car.

Chapter Nine

■◆■

"Move up to the front seat," Juniper said as he opened the back door, "so I won't feel like I'm an Uber driver."

"I think I ought to just stay here at my parents' home tonight," Luciana said as she climbed out. "I don't want to put you out any more than I have already."

"If you really don't want to put me out, you'll get in. Otherwise, I'll have to pick you up and put you in. Now that would be putting me out." He grinned at her to show he was joking. *Or am I? It wouldn't be so bad to have an excuse to have her in my arms again.*

"Which way?" he asked as he pulled away from the curb.

"Do you know how to get to what they call 'Old Town'?" Luciana said.

"Certainly. That's where I'm working now."

"Really? Where? What are you doing?"

"Remodeling a block of buildings on Old Main Street. I'm working with my brother-in-law, Paul Keaton. He's the architect on the project."

"Yes, I remember you saying that when you brought Roscoe and me home, but I didn't realize that's where your project was located. That's not far from my office." She shook her head. "Seems like you're always rescuing me."

"I'm glad I'm around when you need rescuing," Juniper said.

"Well, I hope this doesn't get to be a habit."

"What? Me rescuing you?"

"No. My needing to be rescued," she answered.

After a short distance on the loop of highway that circled the town, Juniper exited. The area was quite different from the elegant neighborhood he'd just left. When he turned off the main thoroughfare, the streetlights became dimmer and farther apart. Few businesses were still open: a liquor store here, a bodega there. The drugstore, the furniture store, the pawn shop——those owners had long since locked up and gone home.

"I wouldn't expect you to be living in this area," Juniper said. *Your family obviously has money. I'd think you could afford to live in a better area.*

"It's close to work, and my clients live around here. If I lived out in the 'burbs, or in the part of town where my parents live, they'd think I was from another world, and they wouldn't confide in me. I feel closer to them, living in the same neighborhood."

"Your clients? Where do you work? What do you do?"

"Ever hear of Haven Home?"

"Umm . . . it sounds familiar, but I don't know what it is."

"It's a place where people in trouble, especially women, can come and get help or advice," Luciana said. "Turn right at the next corner."

It's beginning to make sense. "The battered wife?"

"Yes. The battered wife," she said. "This was by far the worst I'd ever seen."

Juniper was quiet, waiting for her to continue. When she

didn't, he prompted, "And the husband's in jail?"

Luciana nodded.

"That's why you were there . . . at the jail—when you said what you did, about seeing that someone stayed locked up—— you were talking about the husband."

"Yes."

"But he won't stay locked up forever, will he? That is, he'll be out on bail, right?"

"Hopefully, the bail will be high enough that it'll take a while for him to come up with it, and by then. . ."

"And by then what?" Juniper prompted.

"By then, maybe I'll have her out of the hospital and hopefully out of town." She sighed. "At the next corner, turn left. It's the big apartment house on the right."

As he followed her directions, thoughts were bouncing around in Juniper's head like balls in a pinball game. Questions he wanted—no, needed—to ask.

"How badly is she hurt?"

"Pretty bad," Luciana replied. "Nose broken. Both eyes swollen shut. One rib cracked. A couple of fingers broken—he deliberately broke them when she was trying to pry his hands from around her arm. Bruises all over."

"Why? I mean . . ."

"Why indeed? Why does a man beat his wife almost to death? Because he didn't like what she fixed for dinner? Because he had a bad day at work? Because he had a lousy childhood? If a neighbor hadn't called the police, she would've been dead instead of badly injured. If I wasn't here, helping and arranging things and giving her courage, she'd go back to him so he could do it again."

"Go back to him?" Juniper said as he pulled to the curb in front of the big brick apartment building. "You've got to be kidding."

"Kidding?" She shook her head. "No. I'm not kidding. These women, these battered wives, that's what they do. It's what she's done before."

"Why? Why would she go back to someone who treats her that way?" *There's not a woman I've ever met who would put up with that kind of treatment. Witches don't put up with stuff like that. Why do ordinary women?*

"Because . . .," she sighed once more, and leaned back against the headrest, and despair was in her voice. "Because there's no place else to go. Or because they can't . . . or think they can't . . . make it by themselves. Or because they've been brainwashed into thinking that they're trash and deserve the beating. That if they only could behave the way their husband or boyfriend tell them to, then they won't get beat up."

"That's a bunch of crap."

"To you, maybe, and to me. We who were raised in happy homes see that. To women who were raised in homes where this is the norm, where their father beat their mother, this is how families act." She smiled in the dark. "We don't know how lucky we are." She reached for the door handle.

"I'm walking you to your apartment," Juniper said as he opened his door.

Chapter Ten

■◆■

ALTHOUGH HE HAD never met her, Juniper couldn't get the visualization of the battered woman out of his mind. It entered his dreams. It popped into his head at the most inconvenient times. He'd heard the term 'abused wife' before, of course. Most people have if they read the newspapers or watch TV. But he hadn't dwelt on it. Hadn't actually formed a vision of what Luciana had described. Hadn't thought of the severity, the brutality, or the why of the situation.

Both eyes swelled shut. A cracked rib that made it agony to breath. A body bruised and beaten, black and blue. Now that Luciana had described it, his body shivered in empathy, as if he were feeling the suffering himself, or if it had happened to his sister. That a man would do something like that to a woman—any woman—much less the woman he supposedly loved, was beyond Juniper's understanding. It plagued his thoughts, leaving little room for thinking about the job he was employed to do.

On Old Main Street, the clients were beginning to move into their new shops and homes. Since they were all witches, or at least magickal creatures of some sort, one would think that they could design and achieve whatever interior they needed or wanted. This, however, was not true. Special people, witches or sorcerers or such, are just like ordinary folks. That is, they have their own talents and gifts, which in some cases are limited to a very narrow path. Some can control the weather. Others can produce fire, or talk to animals. They turned to Juniper for his talent in interior design. They told him what they wanted it to look like, and he made it happen.

The shoemaker could make all sorts of magickal shoes and boots. Dancing shoes, running shoes, jumping shoes, even shoes that could render people invisible. He could make them. But plan his shop? Left to him, it would be a jumble of pieces and parts. It was up to Juniper to produce the perfect space. The old man grumbled and groused as Juniper's magick yielded first one showroom, then another. He would've been content—or at least as content as any troll can be—working from a cave. But you can't sell many shoes, even magick shoes, from a cave.

And there was his wife to please as well. She was not a troll. A gnome, possibly. Or even a large pixie. She was a pleasant person, short, like her husband, but as smiling and congenial as her mate was growling and disagreeable. Juniper thought of her as a plump dumpling of a woman, with gray hair pulled back into a bun, rosy cheeks, and piercing blue eyes that could see truth or lies a mile away. Her old-fashioned dresses, sewn from gently patterned gingham, were always covered by a white apron.

Juniper was working on their living quarters above the shop, producing a home that met her expectations, when his mind grasped the implications of two such diverse personalities living together. "Does he ever get angry with you?" he asked the dumpling.

"Angry? With me?" she smiled as she stood contemplating

whether to leave the arrangement of the parlor as Juniper had magicked it. "No. Not with me. With the rest of the world, maybe. But not with me." She laughed as she picked up a sofa pillow and fluffed it. "He knows I'm the only person who'd put up with him, you see." She set the pillow back where it had been. "This is just right, Juniper. Just exactly what I had in mind."

"So he's never . . . that is . . . ever . . ." Juniper couldn't quite get the question out.

"Ever what? He's never what?"

"Hit you?"

"Hit me?" She looked dumbfounded at the thought. "Never. No, never. He wouldn't. He loves me, you see." As she spoke, they walked into the roomy kitchen, magicked according to her directions. She twisted a fold of her apron as she talked. "He doesn't say it out loud, like, but I know it by the way he treats me. Buys me sweets, he does, and rubs my back when I'm tired. If he goes walking in the woods, he'll bring me back a little pretty. Maybe a leaf all red and yellow, or a wildflower to put in a vase." She looked embarrassed to be talking about love.

"And I love him as well. I fix his coffee just the way he likes it, and make those cookies, ginger crisps." She sniffed. "Don't like ginger crisps meself, much, but I make 'em 'cause they're his favorites."

"What would you do if he did? Hit you, that is." Juniper could barely blurt out such a question, but he needed answers. Answers from magickal people. Were they different from ordinaries in this matter?

"Leave him, of course." She looked amazed that he could ask such a thing. "I'd never put up with that. Never."

"Where would you go?"

"To one of the children." She looked a million miles away, thinking. "Yes. I'd go to one of the children." She nodded her head. Pulling herself back to the present, she said, "But he'd never hit me. Never has. Never will." She looked around the room. "Juniper, you have this just right. Just like I wanted it, to a tee." She turned and hugged him. "Thank you, dear boy, for our new home."

"You should thank the Pellegrinos for the home. They're the ones who came up with the idea for this block of shops for the community. They're the ones you pay your rent to," Juniper said as he leaned over to hug her back.

"But you're the one who made it look like this—like my dream home. I could never have done it myself. Thank you."

From there, he went down the block to the bookstore. Pausing on the sidewalk, he admired his handiwork before going in. The entrance looked old, like the stone doorstep had been placed there a hundred years ago or more and had been worn smooth by generations of readers coming to find the book they fancied. The facings around the windows appeared to have been crafted not long after the city was founded, the dark green paint covering a multitude of nicks and gouges. The sign above was simple. *Books for Sale* it announced. That's all the bookseller had wanted. "Magick," she had said, "that's what will bring the shoppers in. If the book they need is here, magick will draw them in. If they want the latest best-seller, the *au courant* read, they will pass on by. That's the way I want it."

On the outside, on either side of the doorway, sat a concrete urn, filled to overflowing with bright red geraniums, which were repeated in the planters hanging outside the upstairs windows. The cheerful flowers transformed what might have been a drab exterior to a welcoming one. Through the many-mullioned window, stacks of books could be seen by passers-by. *I know things,* the shopfront shouted. *I hold secrets. Come in and I'll share them with you.* Juniper went in.

"Juniper!" the woman said. She abandoned the books she was shelving. "I'm so delighted with my shop. Thank you, thank you, thank you." She reached out and took his hands in hers.

In her youth, in another time and another place, she could have been a princess. Auburn hair was piled on top of her head, glints of red promising a hidden glory if it were to come tumbling down. If one looked closely, wrinkles were beginning to form here and there, but they did nothing to detract from her beauty. They only added character to it. She looked like what she was—an expat, a refugee from a noble family, with secrets buried deep, still elegant as befits a member of royalty.

"I've already had a customer," she chortled. "Already. Can you believe it?"

"Really? I'm happy people are finding your shop," Juniper said.

"A young woman wanted a book on the powers of gemstones, and I was able to take her right to it."

"Of course you were." Juniper smiled. He wanted to ask if she had books to help abused women, but he didn't quite know how to ask that. "How about your living quarters? Are they what you wanted?"

"Yes, they are. Just blank. I prefer to furnish them myself, one piece at a time, as I told you. What I'm meant to have will call to me. I bought a bed. A plain bed. For everything else, I'll put it out to the universe, and the universe will send me to the right place, to the right thing. For now, all is perfect. For now, I live in anticipation, and life is good."

A perfect mantra—I live in anticipation, and life is good, Juniper thought as he walked to his car.

Chapter Eleven

．◆．

WHEN JUNIPER finally found Haven Home, it was a non-descript storefront in a row of other equally forgettable businesses. Nothing on the exterior gave any clue as to what it was about. No signs. No pictures. Just 'Haven Home' in black letters trimmed with gold on the plate glass window. Luciana had said it was somewhere close by, so Juniper drove around looking for it when he'd determined that he had to do something to settle his thoughts. He wanted . . . no, he needed . . . to talk to Luciana again. Talk about these women who allowed themselves to be beaten half to death and then still went back to the abuser. Why? Who were these women? What made them think the way they did? How and why was Luciana involved in their lives?

He had started the morning with the shop owner of the Cup and Leaf Tearoom, the newest business to start moving in on what the Pellegrinos were calling "the special block."

"Hiyo, Juniper," the woman behind the counter said when he walked in the door.

"Hiyo, Alfreda," he replied as he gathered the slight figure in a hug. He didn't know much about the diminutive woman, except that she was unreservedly friendly with everyone she met and enthusiastic about the prospects of a whole neighborhood of mystical shops, hers in particular.

"Let me fix you a cup of tea. I got a bunch of new varieties in first thing this morning." She went behind the counter and rummaged through the boxes setting on the back bar. "How about blackberry sage? Or here's a really special one, milk oolong. Let me make you a cup of that." She went to work without waiting for his answer.

Juniper strolled around the room. "Anything else you need me to do around here? Need more tables? More chairs?" The room looked sparsely furnished to him. He frowned as a looked around.

"Not for now," Alfreda said. "I don't want it too crowded. It should look more like a living room. It is a living room—my living room. I can let you know later, after I start having customers, if I need more seating." She placed a mug on a small, round table in front of the big multi-paned window looking out onto the street. "Do you use sugar?"

"No, thank you," Juniper replied, taking a seat. "I take it plain."

"Good for you," Alfreda said. "I gave it to you in a mug. It seems more manly than a teacup."

Juniper smiled at that and took a sip of the concoction she served him. "Hmm. Delicious," he said. "It tastes like you added milk."

"That's why it's called milk oolong," Alfreda answered. "Nothing added. It's a special tea, grown in Taiwan, and it tastes like milk naturally."

"I like it," Juniper said, taking another sip.

"It helps regulate the metabolism," she said, "and to keep weight down." She chuckled. "Not that either you nor I need to worry about that." She took a sip from the rose patterned china cup in front of her. "It's also good to keep clear skin, and I don't know a woman alive who isn't interested in good skin, so I ought to sell a lot of it."

"I imagine you will," Juniper commented as he looked around the room. "I don't remember the room being exactly like this when I left the other day," he said, frowning.

"Oh, I moved a few things around. I hope you don't mind."

"It's your shop," Juniper said, surprised. "You can do anything you want with it. I'll be glad to move things for you, though, when you want them in a different place."

"That's no problem," Alfreda said. "That's one talent I do possess. I can shift objects from one place to another. Weight doesn't matter."

"Oh . . ." Juniper pondered that. He wasn't quite sure exactly what mystical category Alfreda fit into, but he'd bet that if all those blond ringlets were pushed aside, pointed elfin ears would be visible. Elves were notoriously strong in spite of their dainty appearance, besides having some magickal ability as well. "Well, is there anything else you need for me to do while I'm here?"

"Juniper, I think you have magicked the perfect tea shop. This . . ." she said as she looked around, "is my living room, and it's just as I wanted it, as is my bedroom, and the bath, and the kitchen. I enjoy tweaking everything. Add a little here. Take a little there. Adjusting it is half the fun.

"As soon as I get the teas all set up, and some cookies baked, I'll open for business. I'll sell tea by the cup or pot, and supplies to brew it at home. We'll have a friendly atmosphere, so folks will want to sit and visit. We may even have meetings."

"Meetings?" He hadn't heard anything about meetings.

"Yes. Maybe book clubs or discussion groups. Whatever interests people. What they might want to talk about."

"Politics?"

"Maybe, especially if it affects women. Oh, yes, Juniper. There is one more thing if you could conjure for me, please."

"Certainly. What is it?" he asked, setting his now empty mug on the table. He looked around at the comfortable chairs and loveseats, all with a handy table near at hand for a cup or plate.

"Some shelves to display tea pots for sale."

"Easy. Where do you want it?"

"I think right there," she said, pointing to a section of wall on the far side of the room.

Juniper closed his eyes, forming the vision in his head, then opened them and, pointing a finger at the spot she'd indicated, frowned. A tall, wide set of shelves appeared.

Alfreda clapped her hands. "I always get a thrill seeing magick," she said. "That's just what I wanted. Thank you."

"You're quite welcome," Juniper said. "And now I must be going. If you need anything else, make a list. I'll come back by in a few days."

When he left the Cup and Leaf, Juniper drove back to where he'd spotted the place Luciana had mentioned—the place where she worked. *Haven* means a place of safety . . . escape from harm, and *home* is a place to live. Are there enough people—women—who need a safe place to go to escape maltreatment that there's an agency to help them? Surely they don't live there in that store-looking place.

There's only one way to find out, Juniper told himself. Go inside and ask questions.

Images of a battered woman, eyes swollen shut, bent over around a broken rib, kept inserting themselves into his thoughts. *I have to remove that image, or else I'll be conjuring up a woman,* he thought. *A painfully battered woman.* Clearing his mind, he closed his eyes, opened them again, pointed his finger and moved his car which was directly in front of Haven Home to a vacant spot in the next block.

Chapter Twelve

．◆．

WHEN HE ENTERED the office, the receptionist looked distinctly
ill-at-ease, as did the woman sitting in one of the orange plastic
chairs lined up against the wall. The one at the desk put one hand
on the telephone, as if to be ready to snatch it up and call for
help if needed. The younger woman sitting in the shabby seat put
her arm around the toddler standing at her knee and pulled him
up into her lap, enfolding him, sheltering him.

"May I help you?" the receptionist asked.

"I wonder if I could see Luciana Diez?"

This was met with silence and a cold stare.

"I was told she works here," Juniper said.

"Who told you that?"

"She did."

"Miss Diez told you she works here?" She studied him over
the top of her glasses. Her expression told him she didn't believe
a word he said.

"That's right. She did," he said firmly. Juniper usually had
better luck than this charming ladies. He smiled. He couldn't

believe that he was being coldly shut out. He watched as she picked up the telephone receiver and punched in three numbers.

The receptionist was older than Luciana by a couple of decades, he thought. Her satiny skin and twists of bead-adorned hair were the same shade of dark brown. She reminded Juniper of a teacher he'd had once. He remembered that he couldn't get anything over on her, either.

"There's a man here to see you," she said into the receiver. "What's your name?" she asked brusquely, as if she expected him to either lie or refuse to answer.

"Juniper Penn."

"He says it's Juniper Penn," she related, but her voice sounded like she didn't believe it for one minute.

When she put down the receiver and looked at him, her attitude was more friendly, but only slightly. "Have a seat. She'll be with you when she can."

Too antsy to sit, Juniper chose to read the posters adorning the walls. There was one urging the reader to get their GED, promising jobs were available to those who had their high school diploma. Another was touting the benefits of joining the military service, while one more advertised the food pantry available at a local church. A cork board held messages and announcements thumbtacked randomly over the surface. Items for sale. Kittens to give away to good homes only. Daycare at reasonable rates. Rummage sale with lots of baby clothes at cheap prices. Some notices were so old they were yellowed and curling at the edges.

When the receptionist didn't called anyone to have Juniper removed, the waiting woman stopped looking so frightened and allowed the wiggling child down again. He stood holding onto her knees, staring at Juniper as he took a seat in one of the scruffy plastic chairs on the other side of the room. Juniper smiled and waved his fingers at the tot. The toddler finally smiled back and waved one hand vigorously. His mother gave

Juniper a dirty look and snatched the child back onto her lap.

Finally, a door on the back wall opened and Luciana came into the room. She saw Juniper immediately, but held up one finger to stop him as he stood up. She turned to the waiting woman. "Cathy, take this note and go to Saint Andrews Church over on Broadview. You know where it is?"

"Yes, ma'am, I do."

"They'll help you get your power back on. They have a food pantry, and you can get some groceries there. You need to come in next week and talk about making some arrangements for child care so you can go back to work. Hear?"

"Yes, I hear. I will, I promise." She took the slip of paper that Luciana held out. "Thank you."

"Lucy, you have two phone calls to answer," the receptionist said, holding out two pink slips of paper.

Lucy? "Lucy?" The nickname slipped from him. The woman who stood before him in jeans and a tee-shirt emblazoned "They say that I'm a dreamer" around a big, yellow daisy was most certainly more suited to being a Lucy than a Luciana.

"Okay. I'll see to them in just a minute," Luciana, or rather, Lucy, answered as she took the memos without looking at them. "Is something wrong? Has something happened?" she asked Juniper. "Is my grandmother okay?"

"No, nothing has happened. I just thought I might take you to lunch," he replied.

"Lunch?"

"You know, that time in the middle of the day? When people usually eat?"

"Yes, I know what lunch is. I'm usually too busy to eat."

"When you're busiest, that's when you need sustenance. Fuel to keep you going."

"That's what I tell her," the receptionist said.

"Does she listen?" Juniper asked.

"Naw. Sometimes she brings herself a sandwich, but most times she forgets. No wonder she's nothing but skin and bones." Her hefty size indicated that she didn't forget to eat.

"Then I think she ought to take time for a good meal, don't you? So she can work better this afternoon," Juniper said.

"I think you're right."

"I think you two better stop talking about me," Luciana said.

"Yes, ma'am, Miss Lucy," Juniper agreed. "We will if you agree to come to lunch with me."

She glanced at the notes in her hand. "Let me answer these first, then I'll go with you."

"Okay, but don't get tied up and forget I'm waiting," Juniper said.

"I won't," Lucy responded, going back through the door she had come from a few minutes earlier.

"Will wonders never cease. You got her to do something for herself, for once."

"Don't speak too soon," Juniper said. "I don't have her out of the office yet." He smiled at the woman who was proving to be his ally. Extending his hand, he said, "Juniper Penn."

"Ophelia Jones," she said, shaking his hand. "Glad to meet someone from Lucy's other life."

"Glad to meet you as well—someone from this life. Ophelia, huh? Your mother was a . . ."

"Father. My father read Shakespeare. It was down to either Ophelia or Desdemona. He said I needed something to liven up Jones."

"Desdemona wouldn't have been bad. In my family it's flower and tree names," Juniper said.

"Juniper is a nice name. Has a ring to it. I'm glad I wasn't Desdemona. I would have ended up being called Desi. Can you just imagine? Lucy and Desi working together again?" Her laughter pealed in waves of amusement and pulled him into the enjoyment of the silly thought.

She got up and walked around to his side of the desk. "Does my heart good to see Lucy in the company of a fine looking young man. I know her family don't agree with her working down here. They think it's dangerous."

"Is it?"

"Might could be," she said as she ambled toward the front window. "Might could be." She stopped and peered out the dirty window. "All hell and damnation!" she yelled out. "The dirty, no-good, son-of-a-skunk. Blast and double blast. Somebody done gone and stole my car!"

Juniper moved to stand beside her. "Where was it parked?"

"Right in front. Right there where that fancy-schmantsy car is parked. I got here early just so's I could park where I could keep an eye on it. Some no-good low-life stole the radio out of it a couple of months ago, and I been watchin' over it ever since then." She shook her head. "And they stole it anyway. The whole dad-blamed vehicle/.

Juniper decided he better fix the situation the best he could. "That's my car in front now," he said as he headed toward the door. "That place was empty when I pulled in it." *Of course it was! I'd moved your car to the next block.*

He went out onto the sidewalk with Ophelia close behind him. "What kind of car was it? What color?"

"Blue. It was a bright blue Honda," she answered.

Innocently, he scanned up and down the cars on either side. "There's a bright blue Honda parked there in the next block," he said innocently. "Maybe you parked down there this time?"

"No sir. I didn't park nowhere else but right in front . . ." She trailed off. "That do look like my car." She took off running.

She came back a minute later. "Don't that beat all. Someone done stole my car and brought it back."

"Does it look damaged in any way?" He squinted his eyes, blinked, and her old Honda had a protection spell firmly in place. *Nobody would ever mess with Ophelia's car again. Except him. If needed.*

Chapter Thirteen

■ ◆ ■

"This is so good," Luciana said, spearing a green bean with her fork. "Better than I usually have for lunch . . . if I eat lunch at all."

"You skip lunch often?" Juniper asked.

"Sometimes, if I forget to bring a sandwich to work with me." She stirred the gravy covering the steaming meat.

"Can't you leave and go eat somewhere?" Juniper was curious about what, exactly, kept her tied to the office.

"Sometimes I could," Luciana said, as she cut a bite from her open-faced hot roast-beef sandwich. "But I don't like to eat at places like this by myself," she looked around the diner, "and I don't care to eat fast-food more than occasionally. It's easier just to skip lunch altogether." She ate the bite of beef smothered in brown gravy, and her eyes closed in appreciation. "Mmm. So good."

So maybe I need to come get you at lunchtime more often, Juniper thought. *Just so you don't starve to death.* He smiled at the thought of dragging her out to lunch despite her protests, like he had today.

"What are you smiling about?" she demanded.

"A happy thought."

She eyed him as she sipped her water. "Happy thoughts are good, I guess." She picked up her fork and moved some of the gravy onto the remaining blob of mashed potatoes. "We don't have enough happy thoughts where I work," she said as she scraped up the last bite.

"What is Haven Home, exactly? That is, what do you do there?"

Propping her fork on her plate, she steepled her fingers in front of her as she studied him. "We help people," she answered, watching Juniper's face. "Especially women and children."

He wondered what kind of response she expected from him, if any. *Wouldn't anybody be sympathetic? Compassionate?* "Like the woman who was waiting for you?"

"Cathy? Yes, like her. Her husband left her, ran off with another woman, and there's no money coming into the household. Her attorney is trying to get child support, but even with that, it won't be enough. She can't sit around crying. She's got to get out and find a job."

"Will she be able to?" Juniper asked.

Luciana's forehead wrinkled in thought. "It'll be hard to find one that pays enough to help. She quit high school to get married. It's hard enough for women who graduate, especially those who don't go on to get training in something . . . anything." She looked back at Juniper, studying him, before returning to eat the last bite of her food left on the plate. "And it'll take perseverance to get her GED and schooling in some field."

"Are there many women like her?" Juniper wondered.

"Too many," Luciana answered. "Far too many."

"You folks want some desert?" the waitress asked as she started gathering the empty plates. "We have some good looking chocolate pie today."

"That sounds great," Juniper said. "How 'bout you?" he asked Luciana.

"I don't know that I can hold any more," she said, placing her hands on her stomach.

"Try," Juniper said. "We'll have two pieces of chocolate pie," he told the waitress.

"Comin' right up."

"The other night . . ." Juniper started. He picked up his spoon and started playing with it. "That woman you were telling about, the one who was in such bad shape, is she going to be okay?" He'd wondered about the situation ever since he took Luciana home that evening.

Luciana sighed. "I hope so. She's out of the hospital, at least, and out of this town. I took her home and helped her pack a bag. I bought a duffel and filled it with things I thought she'd need . . . new clothes, jeans and tees and a couple of dresses. Things she could wear to work. Then I took her to the airport and put her on a plane to California. Her mother's sister lives there and was happy to have Sandra come live with her.

"I talked to the aunt and told her the situation, and Sandra talked to her. I'm hoping she'll settle in out there and not let the husband know where she is. Start a new life."

"Here's your pie, folks," the waitress said as she put mile-high pieces of meringue topped chocolate in front of them. "Enjoy!"

"So you got it worked out," Juniper said, but it was more of a question than a statement. "I'm glad you talked her into leaving."

"Maybe. If she doesn't contact him and tell him where she is," Luciana answered. "And I didn't talk her into it. She decided herself. That's the only way it'll work, if the woman makes the decision on her own."

"Really?"

"Really," she answered. "If I'd talked her into it, it wouldn't last. Even if she left town, she'd be back. She'd get to thinking about it and decide that he wasn't so bad after all, and that he'd change. He'd act contrite, say he'd never do it again. It wouldn't be long until she went back to him, and it would start all over."

"I can't believe a woman would go back to someone who beat her up like that." *There's not a witch alive who would put up with it in the first place. I'd probably feel sorry for a man who even started. If anyone tried it with Ziniyah, she would . . .* He shook his head at the thought of what his sister might do. Turn him into a toad or something.

"Is he still locked up?" he asked.

"For now," she answered, "but not for long."

Juniper's eyebrows raised. "You'd think that anyone who beat up a woman like that would be in jail for a long, long time."

"You'd think so," Lucy answered, "but the problem is, she isn't here to go to court and tell the judge what he did. I could have encouraged her to stay and testify, but he'd be out sometime, and he's done it before and he'd do it again. And he has friends who might think they could help him by taking her out so she couldn't even make it to court. She might end up dead.

"Or I could tell her she was making the right choice, help her get on a plane to the other side of the country and maybe she'll stay there and forget about him. Get a job, find a good man, have a happy life. Picking between the two, which would you choose?"

Juniper shook his head. "I'd pick what you did," he responded, but a feeling of dread had settled over him. It wasn't over, his gut was telling him. It was far from finished.

Chapter Fourteen

■ ◆ ■

DAWN WAS BARELY BREAKING as Juniper stood across the street from the row of businesses he was helping plan. "You want it where?" he asked the man standing next to him.

"Right there," the man said, pointing to a vacant storefront.

"Half that one gone, and half the next one as well. Right?"

"Well, maybe not half of the second one. What we want is a wide walkway, ten feet wide or so."

"Rough brick walls remaining? All the way to the alley?"

"You've got it. You can make it . . . appealing? Interesting?"

"Old world, right?" Juniper asked. "Maybe some vines or something?"

"Something," the man replied. "Can you do that? Or do we need to get a hedge witch back for the vegetation?"

"Let me work with it first. I'll let you know." Juniper frowned. "Josh, want me to do it now? Before we start having any traffic?" He glanced up and down the silent street. The sky was pink, but the sun had yet to peek over the edge of the earth. It wouldn't be long before people started venturing out, starting their days, and the quiet calmness would be gone, replaced by a different energy.

"Sure thing."

Juniper paced a few steps back and forth, looked back across the street at the property in question, and shook his head. Then he straightened his spine, drew himself up, and stretched his arms out to their full length. Pointing all fingers toward the shops in question, he lowered his head, frowned, and wiggled his fingers. Anyone watching might have seen tiny sparks flying from his fingertips, miniature lightning bolts darting forth, then withdrawing. A low rumble sounded, and an alleyway appeared where once had been shops. Jagged edges dropped crumbles of brick here and there before settling, and dust motes swirled.

"Ahh . . ." the man sighed. "Yes. Perfect." He started across the street. "Or it will be."

Juniper followed him. "Some peeling stucco, don't you think?" he asked. "Very old? Maybe a window or two looking down from the second story?"

"Yes . . . yes," the man agreed. "That's what Sabrina wants. Like something from an old village in Europe."

"Doors," Juniper said as they stood close to the altered shops. "There aren't any now. No way to get inside these two shops. Perhaps an angled one here?" He gestured to the left. "Or both?" he said as he turned to the right.

"At an angle here on the corner of this left-hand shop. I'm pretty sure it's going to be an umbrella shop. They didn't want as much space as had originally been there. I'll show this to him this morning and we'll probably sign the lease. Will you be able to work with him today?"

"Sure thing. I can make it anything he wants."

"I'll call you," Josh Pellegrino said, "the old-fashioned way— by cellphone—and give you the go-ahead to put in what he wants as soon as he commits, gives me a deposit, first and last month's rent, and signs a contract."

"And on the right-hand shop? Angled as well?"

"No. It can be facing front. An old door. An old front, for that matter. I have something in mind for that space, but I need to talk to Sabrina first." He walked back into the space that hadn't been there a few minutes before. "We'll need gates at either end. Ornate iron gates that keep people out, but in a nice way."

"Make them look and wonder what's back there," Juniper said. "And want to walk back to see."

"Exactly. But they can't."

"And what's going to be back there?"

"Ways to get to apartments above and behind the shops," came the answer. "We're going to offer rooms or studios above those shopkeepers who choose to have their living quarters behind their business place rather than above it. No sense wasting the space."

"That's a great idea," Juniper said.

"It was Sabrina's brainchild. I'll work with you on that later in the week. There'll be some passages, stairways maybe."

"I'm thinking that we need inscriptions on either end of the block, with The Pellegrino Block on them. Old bronze plaques," Juniper said. "So old that folks will think they've been here forever."

Josh laughed. "I'll run it by the wife and see what she thinks."

When Juniper walked in the waiting room at Haven Home, a dozen people looked at him. One woman juggled a crying baby and another held a tissue to her eyes, as if fighting tears. Ophelia was on the phone. She looked his way and raised her eyebrows before turning away and continued speaking into the receiver. "I'll have her call you when she can," she said and paused to listen. "Uh-huh. Uh-huh."

When she finally hung up the receiver, she spoke to him. "Lucy's got no time to talk to you today. Half these people out here's waitin' on her. Somebody's home sick today, another out on an emergency call, and ever'thing done fell on her."

"No time to eat, either, I assume," Juniper said.

"You got that right."

"Okay. I'll be back," he said. He headed for the door, but he took time to smile at the women filling the chairs lining the walls. They'd had a rough time about something or they wouldn't be waiting to see Lucy. They needed a smile.

He was back in less than an hour, carrying a large sack in each arm. The aroma wafting from them had everyone still waiting sniffing the air. Depositing them on Ophelia's desk, he said, "Be sure she takes time to eat. There's plenty for you too, and others. I'm guessing that if Lucy doesn't get a lunch break, neither does anyone else."

Ophelia's mouth dropped open as Juniper turned and marched out the door once more, again smiling at the women who were still seated there. Several smiled back, and one gave him a thumbs up.

Chapter Fifteen

■❖■

JUNIPER HAD SPENT the morning working on the newly created corridor. Stucco appeared and disappeared. The passageway changed from straight to meandering and back to almost straight again. It appeared to have curves deep enough to prevent anyone from standing at the iron gate and looking all the way to the alley. He had fun with the illusion that was produced by walls that leaned or tilted and by old wooden supports that gave the impression that a door used to open into another realm at that point. At one place, stone columns framed a sham opening into the back of the right-hand building. It could be made functional if the shop owner desired.

Large clay containers and stone pots along the expanse spilled bright flowers onto the floor. *I may have to get a hedge witch to replant these,* Juniper thought. *I don't know a thing about the dirt they ought to be in.*

When Juniper's stomach made him aware that it was lunchtime, he left his endeavor, excited to tell Luciana about this faux place before he realized that he couldn't share the essence of what made it special with an ordinary person. *But I can still have lunch with her—bring her over here and show her,* he thought. Maybe she'll be able to feel the energy of the place, even if she can't know about the magick of it. When he began to question his feelings about this woman, he brushed them aside. *She's just somebody different from the women I'm used to. I've always thought ordinaries were boring, and now I'm not so sure about that. That's all it is.*

When he was dashed in his objective to spend the lunch break with Luciana, he returned to the work site, conjured a small table and chair, and settled with the fragrant sandwich and bottle of beer he'd bought for himself. As he looked around the area he had so recently magicked into existence, he let the spirit of the place wash over him.

It needs an even walking surface, but not one that appears too perfect. He tried tiles in various designs—old patterns he remembered seeing in Italy or Greece. He'd take a bite of succulent beef and cheese and ruminate over the chi of the place before he changed the pathway yet again. He made it look newer. Then older. Then brick. Finally, stones that looked more uneven than they really were. *That's it for now. I can always change it later if I decide I don't like it,* he thought as he wadded the paper sandwich wrapping and put it back in the sack.

He was drinking the last few drops of his beer, gazing up and thinking about vines and flower boxes and lighting when a voice called out to him.

"Hello? Mr. Penn? Alf Birtwistle here. I believe I'm to see you about my shop?"

The man standing at the ornate iron gate which blocked the entrance from the sidewalk was short, balding, and spoke with a hint of a British accent.

Juniper stood. "Ah yes, Mr. Birtwistle. Josh Pellegrino called earlier to say you'd be coming by." He went to the entry and pushed open the elaborate swirls of metal. He went out of the passageway onto the sidewalk. Shaking hands with the man, he said, "You're renting this building, I believe?" He gestured toward the angled double doors leading into the small shop.

"Yes. Yes, indeed I am. Perfect," he said. "Absolutely perfect for what I need. I was so pleased to learn," he glanced around to be sure nobody was nearby, "that such a special area is being formed here in this city. There's one in London, you know, but I'm pleased to live here in America at this point in my life, and in this city. So I'm beside myself to be able to pursue my occupation alongside like-minded individuals."

"And what is it that you do?" Juniper asked as they entered the building. "That is, what kind of a shop are you going to open?"

"Umbrellas," Birtwistle said. "That's my specialty. Umbrellas."

"Umbrellas?" Juniper questioned.

"That's it. I can supply you with any kind of umbrella you might wish or need, but what I can't do," he said, looking around, "is make the shop into what I desire."

Juniper couldn't imagine making a living off a device to keep the rain off your head, but that wasn't his business. "That's why I'm here. You tell me what you envision, and I'll see if I can supply it."

"Just so," Birtwistle said. "That's what I paid the big bucks, as you Yanks say, to get."

For a split-second, Juniper had a horrible thought that he'd be stuck with a client who was impossible to please, like the couple he'd abandoned the day he met Luciana. Unbelievably, they'd thought the condition Juniper had left their home was the latest in avant-garde style from the renowned designer Juniper Penn. They bragged about it and had parties to show off the climbing wall. They provided their guests maps to find the bathrooms, and escorts to locate the exits when the party was over. They were delighted with what Juniper had wrought. Another tour de force for the famous interior designer.

Have faith, Juniper told himself. *Surely I can provide what this man wants. Umbrellas can't be that hard.* And it wasn't. By the time the afternoon was over, the walls were covered with changeable paint which Alf (he insisted Juniper call him by his first name. "We're going to be friends—I can tell," he said) could change from blue to any color he wished with only a touch. There were chains hanging from the ceiling that easily raised and lowered. An umbrella was hung from a hook on the end of each and could be retrieved easily with the touch of a finger. Birtwistle fetched a box from the boot of his car and hung a dozen "brollies", as he called them. "I'll work tonight," he told Juniper, "when there's nobody around. Drop by tomorrow and you'll see. This is enough to know it's going to work like a top." He folded his hands together and hummed as he walked around the room.

They went into the back of the building, where Juniper magicked a cozy bed-sitter and bath. "This is just what I need," Alf declared. "I'll be eating most of my meals out. As long as I have a tea kettle, I'll get along."

"If you decide you need more room, talk to the Pellegrinos about it. They're going to have some apartments, I believe. You could probably rent one here in the block somewhere and be handy. Possibly the one over your shop if it isn't already spoken for."

"That's nice to know. I have a son who lives here in the city," he looked away in thought. "It would be brilliant if he could live near me." He shook his head, sadly, Juniper thought.

"How about a little outside room?" Juniper asked. "I've just now developed the area where I was sitting when you came today. I could give you a door that exits to it, instead of the one you have that opens onto the back alley. As long as you have an exit in the rear of the premises for fire purposes, the city will be happy with it."

"That would be lovely," Alf said, perking up once again. "Can I have a window onto the alley as well? And one onto the passageway, mayhap?"

"Sure thing," Juniper said, and magicked the arrangement.

"Well, all we lack now is the outside," Juniper said. "Traffic dies down this time of day. People are off work and most have gone home. Let's see what we can do." They walked through the shop and out onto the vacant sidewalk. "I can handle this," he said. Looking first to one end of the block, then the other, barriers suddenly appeared, blocking what little traffic might come along. There would be no one to see the magickal appearance of signs or other accoutrements.

"Now then," he said to Alf, who stood next to him looking at the front of the new shop. "What color? What material?"

"Material? Like . . . stone? Wood? Stucco?"

"Yes, like that."

"Stucco would be brilliant. I like stucco. And I like a gold color. Soft gold. No. No. Deep gold."

"The double doors—they okay?"

"Yes. I like the brown and the old looking wood. Maybe some dark green trim around the windows?"

"Done," Juniper said, and the door and a window on either side trimmed in green adorned the deep gold exterior. "I think all it lacks now is a sign to tell people what you sell."

"A long sign," Alf said, his hands spread wide. "Black. Shiny black, with a black frame. The name in gold. *Bumbershoots.* That's what it should say. *Bumbershoots.* Very stylish, you understand. So folks know it's a classy place."

Juniper pointed, and it was done.

"Planters by the door?"

"Yes, please."

Juniper produced a planter on either side, each holding a small green bush.

"Very posh," Birtwistle said. "You make it look so easy. I wish I had a bit of your talent."

"If I may ask," Juniper said. "what exactly is your gift?"

"Umbrellas," Alf said, smiling. "Umbrellas are my talent."

Chapter Sixteen

■ ◆ ■

JUNIPER WAS STANDING across the empty street, surveying what he'd accomplished in the area that was beginning to be known in the city as The Restoration on Old Main. He looked to each end of the block, nodded, and the barricades keeping traffic from the area while he was magicking the front of Bumbershoots, disappeared. Now he observed what had been created these last few days.

At the far left end, the first two shops were still the plain yellow brick exteriors they'd started with. Vacant for now, it wouldn't be long before they were occupied by a magickal business of some sort. Between them, a narrow door promised access to the upper floor. He wasn't sure the entry was visible to everyone or only to members of the mystical community. He'd need to check that out. The third store was occupied by the cantankerous cobbler. White clapboard siding held a dark green sign lettered with gold. It stretched above the large window and announced 'Rupert Hawtrey—Shoemaker.' A smaller board propped inside the glass declared, 'handmade custom shoes guaranteed to fit.'

What it didn't say, but was assumed by the magickal clients who would be ordering Mr. Hawtrey's products, was that the hand-fitted, hand-tooled, spell-filled shoes would be very expensive. Shoes for people who won races, dance competitions, and beauty contests despite all prognostications to the contrary didn't come cheap. Neither did shoes that accomplished even more magickal deeds. Shoes that simply looked nice and fit well were more likely to be affordable. Those customers would be able to brag to their friends just as well at a fraction of the price. The shop was dark, but light shown from the upstairs windows, and Juniper could imagine the plump wife of the cobbler serving him supper as they discussed the events of the day.

Next in the row of buildings was another empty shop, and Juniper noticed for the first time the "Rented" sign in the window. *That's probably my job for tomorrow,* he thought, wondering who and what was going to occupy the space. Each day was a surprise for the magickal designer. Always something interesting—something new—*and I don't have to pop over to another part of the globe to be entertained.*

Following that was the elegant establishment of Madame Agatha Aragon, couturier, although her name did not appear anywhere. Only those who knew who she was and had reason to enter her establishment would be able to do so. Strong magick protected her presence and her identity. Stark white with black trim, the exterior gave no clue as to what was inside. Should one look in the large, many-paned window, they would see only a simple but elegant room, furnished with a couple of comfortable armchairs on a worn oriental rug. If you weren't expected, the door would not open to you. Unexpected customers were not welcome.

'Bumbershoots' came next in line. Juniper could see Alf

Hawtrey scurrying around inside the room that was already filling with brightly colored and patterned umbrellas. A new sign was in the front window: 'Umbrellas for any occasion,' it said. *Why would a witch or other mystical person need an umbrella?* Juniper wondered. *It's easy enough to use a spell or charm to stay dry.* Juniper shrugged his shoulders. Maybe he caters to ordinaries.

'Bumbershoots' was followed by the iron-gated path that led to the alley behind the shops, and after that came the small shop remaining from the formation of the new passageway. Juniper assumed he'd learn in the next few days what he was to make of the space. He started walking that direction, where he'd parked his car before starting to work earlier in the day. Taking Luciana's advice, his vehicle was now an older model, not as tempting to car thieves as the Jaguar he preferred to drive. He could have put a protection spell on it to keep it safe, but preferred to remain low-key, at least until the magick work in the neighborhood was complete. It was hard enough keeping the rapid reconstruction from gaining too much attention without parking a fancy car in plain sight directly in front of where he was working. *Later, when everything is complete, it will be time enough to drive the Jag,* he thought.

As he walked in the direction of 'Books For Sale' and 'Cup and Leaf,' he heard the sound of an unmuffled engine approaching. "Hey, dude!" a voice called out. "You! Good looking!" The raucous voices of several males called out to him. He didn't look their way.

"I'm talkin' to you! You got no manners?" The car idled along beside Juniper as he walked.

Juniper sighed and turned around. Unfortunately, this was something he would have to deal with. A carload of what appeared to be teen-age boys and two giggling girls forced his attention. "These here girls think you're good-looking. Be polite and tell them thank you," the driver demanded. "Don't you think that they're cute too?" He lowered his head and his gaze changed. "Or maybe you don't like girls. Maybe you . . .."

"What I think is that you need to go sober up before you drive anymore," Juniper answered.

"Euwwee, fellers. This handsome dude thinks he's too good-looking for our girls. We need to prove him wrong?" He was answered by the squeals of the girls and "get 'em" and "take him down a peg," along with cursing from the other boys in the car.

Juniper had come to a standstill and stood there thinking about where he ought to deposit the drunken group so they wouldn't get in any more trouble. The tangle of country roads west of the city came to mind, so with a blink of his eyes, the street was once more empty. He hoped they'd blame their intoxication for the fact that they couldn't remember how they got there. Nobody they told about their experience would believe that a strange man walking along Old Main had magickally transported them to the other side of the county.

There was a time, he thought, *when I would've taken them all on in a fight and enjoyed it. It wouldn't have been fair, of course, but . . ..* He wondered if this meant he was growing more mature. He'd stayed in one place for some time, eschewed the party circuit, and passed up a fight. *Maybe I'm growing up.* He smiled to himself at the thought. Mimi would be so proud.

When a car pulled up beside him, his first thought was that his spell hadn't worked. *Nah! My spells always work.* Then he thought it was more troublemakers cruising on a Friday night, until a feminine voice said, "I hoped I might find you still here. I came to say thank you for lunch."

Chapter Seventeen

■◆■

"YOU'RE WELCOME," JUNIPER SAID and frowned. Thinking of the group he'd just dispatched, he added, "but it's not very safe for a woman alone in this neighborhood in the evening."

"You sound like my father," Luciana said, and her own smile turned sour.

"That doesn't make him wrong," Juniper answered. "There was a car-load of mischief-makers by here just a minute ago." He put his hands on her car window so she couldn't roll it back up if he angered her. "I'd hate for them to hassle you."

"I'd be locked up safe in my car," she said as she gave him a cold smile. "What did you do?"

"Told them to go sober up," he answered. *And transported them to where it will take a couple of hours to figure out how to get back to town.*

"Well, I'd know to keep my mouth shut, thank you very much."

"Of course, you would," he said. *Or maybe not. I don't know how good you are at that.* "I just finished work and I'm hungry.

Want to go grab a bite to eat?"

"I'm tired," Luciana said. "It's been a long day. I was going home, soak in the tub, and eat a PB&J for supper."

"I don't care for PB&J myself," Juniper said. "Are you going to make me eat alone?" He tried to put a sad look on his face. "Lucy?"

She looked at him and laughed. "You brought me and the whole office lunch. I guess I owe you a meal. Get in," she said, and he heard the click of the locks releasing.

"You want some more of this soup, Miss Lucy? We got plenty. Let me fill your bowl up again."

"No, thank you, Harold. If I eat any more soup, I won't have room for a piece of pie."

"We don't want that. No, ma'am. What kinda pie you want? I'll go ahead and cut you a slice so's nobody else gets it."

"Chocolate, if you still have some. If not, I'll take coconut."

"I'll take more soup since you have plenty," Juniper said, pushing his bowl toward the side of the table. "It sure is good. Are you the cook?"

The grizzled African-American man warily took the empty bowl without a word and headed toward the kitchen.

"Harold's wife is the cook," Luciana said. "They're Ophelia's aunt and uncle."

"They seem suspicious of me," Juniper said in a low voice. "Am I doing something wrong?"

"Not a thing," Luciana replied. "They just don't have many white folks come in here to eat."

"You're white, and you're in here," he pointed out, looking around the room and seeing no other faces as pale as his.

"I'm not as white as you are," she answered, putting her arm next to his to compare them. "I'm brown. And I've been in here with Ophelia several times. They're used to me."

Juniper had to think about that. He'd traveled all over the world with his family and friends and had never given much thought to ethnicity, religion, or skin color, except as interesting attributes to various individuals. People were people in their own right, and if he chose not to be friendly with somebody, it was because of their attitude, actions, or opinions, not the color of their skin or their country of origin. He was aware that bigotry existed, but he was usually too busy to think about it. If he was to spend time in Luciana's world, he might be forced to think about a lot of things he'd previously ignored.

Like racism.

And abusive husbands.

"What's happening with the woman you helped? The one in the hospital?"

"I spoke with her today. She's on the mend. Enjoying living with her aunt. When her ribs heal and the bruises fade, she's going to look for a job." Lucy picked up her fork and nervously turned it over in her fingers. "She's going to be okay, I think."

"If you talkin' 'bout the wife of that no-good Doozy Collins, I surely do hope she stay wherever she is and don't come around that bum no more. He a disgrace to the male race. Don't know why the judge done let him out of jail. Anybody that treat a woman that way don't need to be walkin' around loose," Harold said as he placed a steaming bowl of soup in front of Juniper. "I brought you another piece of cornbread to go with that soup." He sounded slightly more pleasant than earlier. At least he spoke directly to Juniper instead of ignoring him.

"Thank you," Juniper said, surprised.

"You welcome," Harold replied. "An' you be extra careful, Miss Lucy. That piece of . . ." he paused and started over. "That Doozy Collins, he tellin' people he gonna hurt you for talkin' his wife into leaving him. Says you gonna pay."

"Bullies talk big, Harold."

"Sometimes they act big too," Juniper said. "I don't like the sound of that talk."

"Me neither," Harold said. "Don't like it at all." He shook his head as he left.

"Let's talk about something else," Luciana said. "I drive by Old Main when I get a chance. I like to see what you're doing, and every time I see it, it' changed. You're really getting things done fast. What's new today?"

Juniper was proud of the way the project was progressing and was only too happy to talk about it, even if he couldn't mention the magick aspects of the restoration of the neighborhood. "Today a new shop moved in. Bumbershoots."

"Bumbershoots? Isn't that British slang for an umbrella? Is that what they're going to sell?"

"That's right. The proprietor's name is Alf Birtwistle."

"Alf Birtwistle. A British sounding name if there ever was one," Luciana said.

"And he has the accent to go with the name. I believe he mentioned being from London."

"And he can sell enough umbrellas to support a business? Or is he going to have other items as well?"

"I didn't ask, but I had the same thought as you. Americans don't use umbrellas that much. At least not enough to have a whole store devoted to them, even if it is a small shop." *And what could be magickal about an umbrella?*

"I don't know that it's as rainy here as it is in London," she commented. "I hope he isn't disappointed in sales. What's happening with the fancy iron gate right next to the umbrella shop?"

"It's a path—a cut-through—to the alley. We just got the gate up today. I worked on it some, but it's not finished. I want to add things to it. Pots of flowers and stuff."

"I hadn't noticed it before," she said.

That's because it didn't exist before today, Juniper thought. "Your eye went to the shop buildings until the gate went up. Before that, there was nothing to look at."

She frowned. "I guess so, but I've been looking pretty closely."

"Here's your pie, Miss Lucy," Harold said as he slid a plate with an enormous piece of chocolate and meringue in front of her. "Can I get you some pie?" he asked Juniper. He still sounded a bit begrudging, but better than when Juniper had first sat down.

"I'll take a slice just like that one." *But I bet I don't get one as big as Miss Lucy.*

He was right.

When Harold placed the check on the table, Juniper reached for it, but Luciana beat him to it. "I told you I was taking you to dinner," she said. "You bought lunch for the whole office." She held the slip close to her chest so he couldn't get a look at it.

"Okay, if you'll let me get the tip."

She thought a moment, then said, "I guess that's okay."

Harold will be pleased, Juniper thought as he slid a bill onto the table.

"I'll take you back to your car," Luciana said as they climbed into her vehicle.

"Then I'll follow you home," Juniper responded.

"That's not necessary."

"It'll make me feel better. You don't want me worrying, do you?" He smiled at her.

"Okay. If you say so."

"So, what are you doing over the weekend?" he asked as they walked to her car. "You don't work do you?"

"No, actually, I usually get the weekend off unless some emergency happens. This time I'm taking a couple of days extra. It's my grandmother's birthday, and my aunt and uncle have flown over from Barcelona to celebrate with us. They're in New York. The whole family is flying up there tomorrow to meet them."

"Sounds like fun." It wasn't beyond Juniper to weasel his way into the family gathering. He thought about it, but with Valentina present it might be uncomfortable. "Maybe we could do something together when you get back. Dinner and movies?"

Luciana gave him a long look. "You and Val . . .?"

"There is no me and Val," he answered. "It wasn't serious in the first place. We've moved on." I just don't want to be in a family group, meeting your aunt and uncle, and have Val tell everyone that I'm a loser."

She thought, unspeaking, as she pulled up beside the older car Juniper was still driving while he worked on the Old Main project. Putting the car in park, she finally said, "That would be fun. Okay. I guess."

"You guess?"

"Well, I wouldn't want there to be any hard feelings from Val. She is my sister, after all."

"There won't be. Val isn't interested in me. She's moved on to bigger fish. Believe me."

"Okay then. We're flying back home Tuesday. You can call me." She fumbled around in the drink holder between the seats and pulled out a card and a pen. She wrote her phone number on it and handed it to him. "I'll be home by early afternoon."

He got out and into his car. As he drove behind her to her apartment and watched as she walked to the door, waving as she went inside, he wondered if he should have leaned over and kissed her goodnight when he got out of her car or if that would've been pushing it.

Next time, he thought. *Next time I will.*

Chapter Eighteen

■ ◆ ■

JUNIPER SPENT THE NEXT few days pondering his life, both his past and his future. Raised in a mystical family of superior magickal ability and unlimited funds, it was lucky, he thought, that he hadn't died a spectacular death like his brother-in-law, making an ordinary car fly while too drunk to attempt such a feat. Juniper had tried some stupid stunts when he was in his teens, but that had ended years ago. His father, Giles, still hopped around the globe, but his nomadic way of life had morphed into adventures like mountain climbing, parachute jumping, cave exploring, and other exploits requiring stamina and bravery. Juniper thought they also likely involved women other than his wife, Mimi, who was much more a homebody. She favored spending most of her time where she could see and talk with her grandchildren and friends daily, preferring people in her local coven over the jet-setting crowd in glamorous places.

Juniper thought he must have more of his mother's Irish genes kicking in. His early twenties had been spent partying in the company of whichever pretty young witch was handy, but now . . .

Is this what people mean when they talk about growing up? he wondered. *Staying in one place? Having pride in one's work? Worrying about other people—and ordinaries at that?*

He spent Saturday designing the shop where the night before he'd noticed the rented sign in window. It was an easy project. An attorney's office contacted him about moving in. They were familiar with Juniper's work, since he'd used his talent in their former place of employment, an upscale firm located in a downtown skyscraper. Three junior lawyers with the elite partnership had decided to form their own agency specializing in the legal problems of the less fashionable community. When they learned the Restoration of Old Main was taking place under the auspices of the Pellegrinos, they gave notice, signed a lease, and picked out a storefront. Saturday morning they met with Juniper to voice their preferences in style and furnishings. It didn't take long for him to magick the reception area, private offices, conference room, and all the other necessities needed to start the new firm in business. It didn't, after all, take the imagination of interactive walls or sound-effects. Just a nice looking office that would appear sharp and modern, but not too expensive. One that would put the clients as ease and assure them that they were in good hands.

Juniper was through with the job early. With no place to go. And nothing to do. He could have joined friends and acquaintances at any of a variety of places around the globe, but he didn't want to. He could have popped in at his mother's home, or his sister and brother-in-law's house. But that didn't appeal either. He wondered what Luciana was doing. He could have searched her out in New York City. It would have been an interesting tracking problem. It would probably weird her out, though. So he tried watching TV and fell asleep on the couch. And dreamed of Luciana.

■ ◆ ■

Sunday morning Juniper met Josh and Sabrina Pellegrino at The Restoration. The focus of their day were the apartments that were being eked out of unused spaces behind and above the redesigned businesses.

"This is a great idea, Sabrina," Juniper said. "You can have several flats of varying sizes. Good use of your space." They'd been walking around the area they were collectively calling Old Main, or sometimes referring to it as The Restoration.

"We already have one person asking. He's a writer and wants a quiet space in an area that will be good for his creativity. Living among other like-minded folks is a plus for him," Sabrina said. "And if we run out of room, we could add a third story here and there."

"Think you could sneak that by the city?" Juniper asked.

"Sure," Josh Pellegrino answered. "Make it look old, like it's been there all along, and any city inspector will frown and call his predecessor a fool for leaving it off the plans on file."

"To tell you the truth," Juniper said, "I've been thinking about it myself. I think I'd like it better here than in the apartment I'm living in at the present."

"I thought you had a posh place downtown," Sabrina said. "Would this be a come-down for you?"

"It would be different, that's for sure," Juniper answered. "But I'm not the swanky person I used to think I was. I like the vibe here better."

"That brings me to something else," Josh said. "Let's go out and sit in the allée and talk."

"Is that what we're going to call it? The allée?" Juniper asked.

"That's as good a name as any," Josh said. "That's what they would call it in Europe."

"I noticed that you have the umbrella shop's back door opening out here," Josh said as they entered by way of the ornate iron gate.

"Yes. I thought it better there than the alleyway."

"It is that," Josh commented. "We need to think about who's going to have access through the gate, though, and enable them to come and go that way."

"We can talk about that later," Sabrina said. "Let's talk business now."

"Business?" Juniper questioned.

"Have you ever given thought to . . .that is . . .would you ever consider . . ." Josh stumbled.

"Juniper, we'd like for you to become a partner in our development company. We've come to the realization that we couldn't do what we're doing without your talent and help. We work well together. We get along. And you have a natural feel for what we and the clients want. Instead of paying you by the job, we'd like for you to share in the profits." Sabrina stopped speaking and Josh took over.

"We know you like your freedom to go whenever you want. This might be too restricting if there's a project underway."

"Josh, don't talk him out of it before we even get started," his wife said. "Juniper, you could still take off when you wanted to, just not in the middle of something important."

"What would it entail," Juniper asked, "besides what I'm doing now?"

"Well, for one thing, if we lose money, you'd lose instead of making money," Josh explained.

"There you go again," Sabrina said. "He's the most pessimistic person around," she said to Juniper. "And witches aren't usually pessimistic."

"Are you making money or losing money now?" Juniper asked.

"Making money on the shopping center on the west side," Sabrina said. "It's too early to tell about Old Main. "But there's no reason to think we won't make money here as well."

"So what would be different in what I do now as an employee and what I would do as a partner?"

"Make decisions," Josh said. "Say yay or nay about things."

"Look for other opportunities," Sabrina said. "Other investments."

"And share the expense as well," Josh offered.

"We want to stay here, in this city, for the near future," Sabrina said. "Until the kids are grown we don't want to be tied up anyplace other than right here."

"We don't want to be traveling———magickally or otherwise——while the children are small," Josh said.

"I can understand that," Juniper said. "My sister, Ziniyah, and I traveled all over the globe with my parents when we were kids, but I can see it's good to have a more settled home life when there are children involved."

"You turned out great," Josh said, "but I've known witches and other special people who haven't. Folks who have no sense of where they fit in—where they're happiest. The world can be a lonely place if you don't have roots to keep you grounded. That matters whether you're an ordinary or magickal."

"So we're going to stay here for the next few years," Sabrina said. "And we'd like you to join us. Form a partnership."

"We already know we work well together," Josh said. "And we'd like to do more projects with you after this one winds down."

"Not exactly winds down," Sabrina added. "Gets full. Gets settled. The little shop at the entrance of the breezeway," she waved her hand toward the street, "that's going to be the office for The Restoration on Old Main. We'll hire a manager, or rental agent, or someone, to oversee everything."

"I thought you'd probably do that," Juniper said.

"We're taking care of the original leasing," Josh said. "But I think it would be a good idea to have somebody onsite, especially with apartments in addition to the shops. I can see right now that it's more fun to develop property than to manage it. I'd rather look for more places to buy and develop. We'd always have the final say," he said, "but not be involved in the day-to-day operations."

"And you would, as well, if you take us up on our offer," Sabrina added. "The three of us would discuss things and come to a mutual agreement on stuff like buying or selling property."

"You might as well know," Josh said, "that we've already been talking about other properties we might like to buy."

"I've been thinking about that as well," Juniper said.

Chapter Nineteen

■ ◆ ■

JUNIPER WOKE UP Monday morning with a sense of excitement bubbling through him that he hadn't felt in a long time. He hadn't given the Pellegrinos an answer the day before, but they all knew he was going to accept their offer of a partnership. "It's just a precaution, a bit of wisdom, to 'sleep on it', as the saying goes. Gives me time to think of all the bad points of the deal, if there are any," he told them. He realized, though, that he saw The Restoration differently this time as he visited the tenants. He was almost, but not quite, the landlord instead of the employee who magicked the premises to be what they wanted it to be.

"Good morning, Mr. and Mrs. Hawtrey," he said as he entered the shoemaker's business. The scent of spice wafted through the air. The unusual couple was sitting in rocking chairs at the rear of the unique showroom. Instead of racks, stacks, and rows of shoes so common in ordinary shoe stores, there were few samples on display under small spotlights in shelves along the walls. Juniper called himself lucky to have gotten the troll to agree to that much.

"Good morning, Mr. Penn," the plump little woman replied. "Come have cookies and milk with us."

"Cookies and milk?" Juniper repeated as he passed the large worktable where the cobbler did his craft.

"I made ginger cookies this morning," she said. "Rupert needs a little pick-me-up by the time he's worked this long."

As it was still early in Juniper's mind, he wondered at what hour the shoemaker started his day.

"Some people don't loll away half the day before they start," Rupert said. "I'd never be finished if it were half noon before I started." His voice implied the words "like you."

"These are delicious, Mrs. Hawtrey," Juniper said as he bit into a cookie. "I can see that cooking is your talent."

"Oh, no," the woman said, and blushed. "I don't have a talent, least ways not like Rupert does, and you. My great-granny, she was a kitchen witch, but the gift wasn't passed along to me. I'm the nearest thing to being ordinary there is." She smiled at her husband. "I just enjoy being in the company of those who do have the talent. I think I'm really going to like living in a neighborhood of special people. It feels good here."

"I'm glad you're happy, Mrs. Hawtrey. Are there any adjustments I need to make while I'm here?"

"More light over my workbench," Hawtrey growled. "It's too blamed dark over there to see anything. And I have orders I need to fill."

Juniper remembered the old troll's orders when the site was first magicked. "Not so many lights. This isn't some operating room in a hospital." But he didn't bring it up. You seldom win arguing with a troll. And if you ever happen to, you'll regret it.

Pointing a finger and blinking his eyes produced an adjustable hanging lamp. "One enough? Or another at the other end?" he asked.

"Might as well have two," Rupert said, "while you're here. Who knows when you'll ever check on us again."

"Here, Juniper," Mrs. Hawtrey said as he readied to leave. "Take a cookie for the road. Take two." He did.

The attorney's office was calm and efficient when he stopped in there. They couldn't come to an agreement about the order of the names on the front glass, or sign, or both, or none. He told them he'd check back and do that job in a day or two, suggesting that they consider making the storefront look old and settled, like an English barrister's office. They said they'd think about it. The red-headed receptionist smiled and flirted and said she'd look forward to seeing him again. Juniper ignored her.

At Bumbleshoots, Alf Birtwistle was helping a customer when Juniper walked in. "We have it in several colors," Alf was saying as the customer turned the umbrella this way and that in his hands. "And we have both the compact model as well as the traditional style you're holding."

The businessman holding a long, black umbrella, furled into a tight column, frowned as he glanced toward Juniper. "And you guarantee it?"

"Indeed, sir, I do. With that bumbershoot on your arm it will never rain upon you."

"Never rain?"

"Never. As long as it's on your arm or in your hand, it won't rain where you are."

"But I don't have to open it?"

"No sir. You don't have to open it for it to work," Birtwistle said. "And that's the perfect model for you. Black. Traditional. We call it 'the businessman'."

"I'll take it," the man said, and the two went toward the small counter and cash register to complete the sale.

"Mr. Birtwistle . . ." Juniper began when the customer left.

"Alf, please, dear boy. Alf."

"Alf, I had no idea that sort of umbrella magick existed," Juniper said.

"I dare say you have no idea of the range and possibilities of brollies—or umbrellas, as you Yanks call them. Someday, when we have time and are in private, I'll demonstrate for you."

"I'd like that. For now, though, is there anything else I can do for you? Anything you need conjured to make the shop or your living quarters complete?"

"Not a thing, dear boy. Not a thing." Alf beamed. "But thank you for checking on me."

Just then, two women entered the shop, and as Alf went to greet them, Juniper looked around the room, where open umbrellas and parasols covered the ceiling. The walls displayed every color, size, and decorative pattern on pegs and hooks and racks. Outside, on either side of the entrance, red and blue and gold hung, gaily swinging in the light breeze, and a sign in the window announced, 'Umbrellas and parasols for every need.'

Juniper stood at the iron gate, looking down the passageway toward the back of the buildings. He had finally gotten the straight passage to appear as if it was twisting and turning. The optical illusion might not be perfect, but it was all he could conjure for the time being. *I can work on it more later.*

The next shop was to be the rental agent's office, with the possibility of an apartment behind. He would put that off until darkness of night would cover the abrupt transformation. Sabrina Pellegrino had given him a picture for a suggestion of what she wanted it to look like. Pink, with a striped awning over the entire front of the shop, an old door, and pots of geraniums. It shouldn't be hard to summon that—later, when nobody would be watching. The interior could wait until whoever would be using it could voice their wants and needs.

Following that was an empty spot, run down and decrepit, it was waiting on a client to choose it for their business. Juniper was already planning the upstairs as part of an apartment, slightly upscale, extending from over the rental office. *Perfect for me, should I decide to move from my current digs.*

The next shop was Books For Sale. It was busy, with several customers browsing among the stacks. There was a woman curled up in a plush chair in the back corner, reading, and the wing-chair at the front of the store held a child engrossed in a picture book.

"Good day, Juniper," the regal shop-owner greeted him. Although she was dressed more casually than the brocade dress she'd been wearing the other day, she still looked stately in jeans and an oversized white shirt. Her hair was piled on top of her head as before, but today much of it was spilling out into ringlets that almost reached her shoulders.

"Good day to you as well," he returned. "It looks like things are going well for you."

"To be sure. Each day has shown an increase in customers," she replied. "Word is spreading about our selection of books."

"That's very good indeed," Juniper replied. "Is there anything I need to do for you while I'm here?"

"No. I think not. Thank you for asking, though."

"If you should think of anything, Madame, I'll be around checking."

"Oh, please, Mr. Penn. Don't address me so formally. There's already one in this community who's already known as Madame. Leave that for her alone."

"As you wish," he answered. "It seems only proper, however, that you should have a title."

"It's been many ages since my name had a title attached to it. I'm only a poor book seller now," she said, sadly. "Just call me Eleanor."

When Juniper entered the Cup and Leaf, Alfreda was serving a group of women seated on the front patio. Laughter filled the air as they chatted.

"Good morning, Juniper," she said. "I hope you're enjoying this lovely day."

"I am, Alfreda. I am," he answered. "And you?"

"I'm quite well, thank you. Go on in and I'll be with you shortly." She turned to her customers. "Let me know what you think of this pot of tea. It is milk oolong tea. And this," she lifted a second pot from the tray to place it on the table, "is called Comfort and Joy. It's traditionally a holiday tea, but I like it year round." She poured into an offered cup and set the china teapot in the middle. "When you're through pouring, put the cozies on and the tea will stay hot." She placed a plate of cookies on the table. "Enjoy."

"I'm just checking to see if I need to do anything for you," Juniper said when she joined him.

"Not a thing, thank you for asking. Everything is going super. It's been so busy I may need to hire a helper."

"That's great," Juniper said. Just then a couple walked in the door.

"Have a seat anywhere," Alfreda called to them.

"I'll be going then," Juniper said.

"Don't you have time to sit and drink a cuppa?"

"Not this time."

"See ya around then," the cheerful blonde said as she started toward her customers.

Five empty shops, Juniper thought as he walked back up the block. *One on each corner and three others. I wonder if the Pellegrinos have any prospects? I hope I wouldn't be expected to find renters if I become a partner. That's not my skill.*

Magicking the façade of the office would have to wait until night, when nobody was around, but the inside could be done without anyone observing the changes mysteriously appearing. Juniper started with the front office, but other than smooth walls, a nice desk and some comfortable chairs, he didn't have a clue about what would be needed. Moving farther back in the building didn't help, since he had no idea if an apartment to live in would be needed or wanted.

He moved the steps to the second floor, conjuring an entrance from the allée to a stairway to the upstairs apartment he was planning. *This will make a nice flat,* he thought as he walked through the space. Away from the sight of observers, he cleaned and arranged, forming rooms according to what he himself would prefer. *Who knows. I might move here myself,* he thought as he worked. With no customer to describe what they wanted, the rooms became informally, luxuriously, comfortable.

The front room overlooked the street in front and the trees lining it. Smooth stucco walls were pleasing, and he added a couple of paintings in the style of French Impressionists. Wide plank, dark wood floors gleamed. A modern kitchen shared the room, with a large island dividing the space from where he placed comfy couches and chairs. He conjured a large television set setting on shelves which covered one wall, but he left the other shelves ready for books and objects of art.

I'll think about that later.

Moving to what would be the next room, Juniper mused about the floor plan for the remainder of the flat. A spacious bedroom holding a king-sized bed, dresser, armoire, and night stands came next. A beautiful oriental rug covered part of the dark wood floors. A large walk-in closet and a bathroom with an entrance from the bedroom and another from the hall leading to the front of the building completed the suite.

I like it, Juniper thought. *And that's what counts right now. If the Pellegrinos want it changed, I'll change it. They ought to be able to rent it the way it is for a tidy sum, if I don't keep it for myself.*

He stretched out on the bed and ran his hands over the soft cotton sheets. *Just to test it out,* he told himself. It was midnight when he woke up.

The perfect time to magick the front, he thought as he descended to the street level. There were no cars on the street, nobody to observe his work, so it didn't take long to make the façade resemble the photo Sabrina Pellegrino had given him. Creamy pink stucco covered the brick, with patches peeling away to reveal gray beneath, giving the appearance of a building rescued from the previous century. A pink and white striped awning stretched the width of the frontage, with the words 'Rooms~Apartments' flowing across the canvas in script. Baskets of pink flowers hanging on the wall added personality to the place, and after studying the result, Juniper added a large pot containing a blooming vine crawling up the wall to the second floor. He started to walk away, but after opening the iron gate with a touch, he returned and conjured a sign in the window. *Closed.*

Chapter Twenty

■◆■

WHEN JUNIPER AWOKE the next morning, he stretched, then lay still, listening to the sounds of the neighborhood. At his apartment uptown in the luxurious Excelsior Towers, there was no sound. It was thoroughly and absolutely shut off from the rest of the city—a private sanctuary for a private man. Here the faint hum of traffic drifted into his space, and birds were singing in the trees lining Old Main Street. He could hear the world beginning to move about.

The merest suggestion of a conversation floated through the window opening onto the allée. He thought it might be Alfreda talking with another resident. He couldn't tell what they were saying, but it was pleasant to hear them. It made him feel at home, among family, although he'd never lived in a home anything like this place. He thought he might move some things over from the high-rise today—settle in for a while to see if he remained comfortable in these new surroundings.

The one thing the luxury apartment had that this one didn't was food. After he showered and dressed, he went looking for breakfast. The down-home cooking Lucy had introduced him to the week before was just what he craved, and he searched for the diner where they'd eaten. It was only a few blocks away, but he wasn't sure exactly the direction she'd taken him the other night. He hadn't been paying much attention to the route she drove.

He slid into his Jag, which was fully protected with a spell to keep it safe. He was tired of driving the junker. It had done its job, first ridding him of Valentina, then of being unobtrusive. It was time to be back in the style he preferred. He felt more himself driving his familiar car around several blocks before finding what he was looking for.

"Hey there, Harold," he said as he slid onto a stool at the counter.

"Hey there, Mr. . ." the older man mumbled to a stop as he placed a menu in front of Juniper.

"Penn. Juniper Penn," he said and extended his hand in greeting. "Call me Juniper."

"Coffee?" The owner was friendlier than he'd been the other evening.

"Yes, please," Juniper answered. "I'll have a stack of pancakes and bacon," he said, and pushed the plastic-covered sheet to the side as Harold poured a steaming cup.

"Well, looky here," Ophelia said as she took a seat on the next stool. "Didn't ever expect to see you here."

Harold was observing with raised eyebrows. "You know this fella?"

"I do. He comes 'round the office time to time," she answered.

"Lucy brought me here for dinner the other night. I had some mighty good soup and cornbread."

"That right?" Ophelia studied his face.

"And pie. I had pie," he added. "Chocolate pie."

"Lucy must like him if she brought him here," Ophelia said to her uncle. "Auntee Rose got any muffins today?"

"You know she do. Blueberry today."

"Gimme one, then. And a carton of milk."

"To go? Like usual?"

"You got it," she answered.

"You eat on the run?" Juniper asked.

"It's not for me," she answered, lowering her voice. "It for the kid Lucy hired to come by every morning before school to sweep the sidewalk and empty the wastebaskets."

Juniper raised his eyebrows as he looked questioningly at her.

"Kid don't have no food at home. Lucy tries to fix it up so's he has something, but he's mighty proud. Won't take a hand-out. We pay him a dollar-fifty and breakfast to work. The dollar-fifty will buy him a school lunch." Harold returned with a small white paper bag and handed it to her. "We're doing good to do that. If he thought it was charity he wouldn't take it. Thank you, Uncle Harold," she said and turned back to Juniper. "Lucy's not here today. She's off with her family."

"I know," Juniper said. "She told me. She'll be back this afternoon."

Ophelia slid off the stool and paused, looking around the room. "I got concerns." She leaned close to Juniper so no one else would hear.

"Concerns?"

"That no good—the one what put his wife in the hospital?"

"Yes—I heard about it."

"He's out of jail and talkin' about what he's gonna do to Lucy for havin' him put there, and for hidin' his wife from him."

"I heard about that as well."

"He's got a bad bunch of friends, and they all snoopin' around, like they lookin' for her. Saying bad things they gonna do. I don't like it. I don't like it at all."

Harold approached with a platter full of pancakes and bacon

and heard Ophelia's remark. As he placed it in front of Juniper, he shook his head. "Bad news. That no-good and his bum friends are bad news," he said in a low voice.

"Thanks for telling me." Juniper looked from Ophelia to her uncle. "I'll see to it. I'll take care of her."

He started eating, thoughts of dire retribution running through his head.

Chapter Twenty-One

■ ◆ ■

WITH SEVERAL HOURS to kill before Luciana would be back in town, Juniper had nothing to do but play. The old Juniper, the one from last year, or maybe even last month, would have magickally relocated to another locale—maybe the Riviera or Rio or some other happening place. The Juniper of today wanted to stay close to where Luciana would be in a few hours. She was safe now, either in New York City or on the flight headed this way. He'd be here when she got home, and he'd figure out what to do about her protection at that time.

First things first, he thought. He moved his clothes and toiletries from his high-rise apartment to the one over the rental office. Might as well be close to the action. It didn't take long to put everything away.

Having contacted all the shop owners the day before, he didn't want to bug them by appearing in their businesses again today. Neither did he want to visit his sister or mother. Either would sense in a minute that something was bothering him and try weaseling the truth out of him, which would be hard, since

Juniper himself wasn't altogether sure what was troubling him so much. *Am I worried about Lucy's safety? I can save her from danger—I know I can. Am I worried about what I will do to the scum-of-the-earth who hurts women? Nah! That won't bother me —whatever I do to him he deserves it. Is it . . ..* He gazed off into space, delving into his inner self, the self he sometimes tried to ignore.

He conjured a comfortable seat in the breezeway and relaxed, watching the passers-by on the sidewalk a few yards away, listening to snatches of conversation. "Look at all the umbrellas." "That was good tea. What kind was it again?" "Momma, what does bumbershoots mean?" "Let's go in the bookstore and see if they have a book about . . ."

Finally, when his butt got tired of sitting, even in a comfortable chair, and he still didn't want to face the fact that he was fascinated with an ordinary woman, he decided to distract himself by playing with the arrangement of the unused spaces above and behind the businesses—the spaces intended to become rooms and apartments for rent.

He amused himself as only a superlative conjurer can. Doors appeared and vanished. Hallways led to where they couldn't. Dead ends became entrances to places that couldn't be. Along the way, he fabricated small gargoyles spouting water into basins and flowers blooming where none had been before, much to the delight of bees and butterflies, and the path between Bumbershoots and the rental office gained a small lizard, sunning itself in a patch of warm light. He walked to the gate opening onto the sidewalk and stood there, admiring the scrolls of wrought iron and absorbing the pleasant ambiance. *It needs lights,* he thought. *It's much too dark at night along here.* So antsy that the precaution that an observer might see him caused no concern, he slowly added street-lights. One at a time, he placed an old-fashioned, black iron lamp-post between each tree.

At dark, they'd come to life, spreading circles of light along the sidewalk, guiding the steps of persons on foot traversing this once neglected part of town. Now that people actually lived along here, instead of avoiding the area as they had in the past, there might be strollers in the neighborhood of an evening.

Satisfied that the placement was to his liking, and nobody was staring or commenting or had even noticed the additions, he returned to his seat and resumed worrying about Luciana.

Checking the time on his phone throughout the day, he finally determined he'd waited long enough. She said early afternoon. This is late enough. He touched the designation assigned to "Lucy" on the phonepad and listened to the buzz that signaled a ring on the other end of the connection.

"Hello? Juniper?" her familiar voice eased a certain amount of nervousness that he couldn't suppress.

"Hey there. Are you back in town?"

"Barely. I'm on the freeway back in. I'll be home in a few minutes."

"In your own car? Or a cab? I should have offered to pick you up."

"My own car. I left it in terminal parking. It's handier that way. Always there when I need it."

Not as safe as if I had picked you up, but what's done is done. Too late for that now.

"Did you have a good time?"

"A wonderful time. The best part was seeing my aunt and uncle and cousins from Barcelona for the first time in a couple of years. We had a ball."

"Sounds like fun. I like getting together with my family."

"I'm worn out. We never went to bed at a decent time. I only got a couple of hours sleep before I had to get up and catch the flight home."

"I was hoping we could go out to dinner," Juniper said, trying to think of any way he could get in her presence.

"Not tonight, I'm afraid. I'm going to bed as soon as I get there. I'll probably sleep until tomorrow."

"Do you have to go to work tomorrow?"

"I will if I feel like it, and I probably will."

"Nobody to fill in when you aren't there?"

"There is now. We've been short-handed for a while, but everyone's back, and they've hired a new person. That's how I was able to take a few days off."

"You work too hard."

"I'm needed." The sounds changed, and he heard her moving around. "I've pulled up at home." The car door slammed. "It's been nice talking to you, but I need to hang up to unlock the . . ."

The sounds he heard next weren't words, exactly. They were more like little screams, shrieks, cut off before they were at full voice. "What . . . oh . . . god . . . who . . ." The sound he heard must have been her phone hitting the ground.

Chapter Twenty-Two

．◆．

TO HELL IF someone sees me disappear or appear. I'll fix it later.

One minute Juniper was in the allée, talking on his phone. The next, he was beside Luciana, gathering her into his arms.

She screamed and jerked back.

"Shh . . .. It's just me," he said, and she relaxed.

"How?" She started speaking, then looked back at the paint-smeared door.

"I was close," he said. "Almost here, so when you screamed, I came." *Not so much a lie. And it's necessary.*

Juniper felt her shaking and pulled her closer. Together they looked at the vulgar words, written on her front door with bright red spray-paint. A barely whispered obscenity escaped his lips as his mind thought much worse. "The guy who beat his wife," he said. "Doozy. And his posse."

"How did you know his name?" She looked up at him.

"Word gets around." He saw the sliver of light around the door. "It's open. He's been inside."

He kept one arm around her while he pushed the door open with the other hand. "Stay back," he said and pushed her behind him as he took a step inside.

It was a shambles. The floor was littered with everything that had once been in the shelves lining one wall. Books and magazines mixed with pencils and pens and pieces of broken china covered the floor. Stuffing spilled out of the couch and chair through the slashes that covered every surface. On the wall behind the sofa, large red letters proclaimed "DIE BITCH," flowing over the framed print that hung there.

In the kitchen area at the end of the room, pots and pans and broken dishes covered the floor, liberally covered with what looked to be cereal, flour, and ketchup. Juniper didn't sense anyone in the apartment, but he urged Luciana to stay behind him just to be safe as they edged into the bedroom, stepping carefully over the debris littering the way.

The sheets had been ripped from the bed, and the mattress had a big, red X on it. Red paint on the wall behind the headboard proclaimed "X is where I do it to U." The drawers had been pulled from the dresser and the contents dumped on the floor.

In the bathroom, there wasn't much to do damage with or on. The old-fashioned medicine chest was open, and a bottle of aspirin had been opened and poured out into the sink, along with the purple liquid from the cough syrup bottle discarded in the toilet. The tiles surrounding the shower again stated, "DIE BITCH."

"Anything missing?" Juniper asked her, straining to hold his voice low and calm, instead of giving way to the fury he felt.

"I can't tell, but it doesn't matter. I didn't have anything of value here anyway. Anything important I left at my parents' home." Her own voice shook as she spoke.

"You have to call the police and report it."

"Yes. I know. That's what I tell my clients. Always report it. Build a history." She took a deep breath and started patting her pockets.

"Here. You dropped it outside, and I picked it up." Juniper handed her the phone he'd magicked into his hand a second earlier. "Let's wait outside in my car," he said. "You can call from there. No use looking at this any longer." He put his arm around her shoulders and urged her toward the door.

Luciana nodded and was edging her way through the living room when she stopped. Pushing aside a lump of foam rubber that had once been a cushion, she picked up a photograph, the frame and glass mangled. Hugging the picture of her family close to her chest, she allowed the tears to spill down her cheeks. Juniper squeezed her shoulder and kept his arm firmly around her all the way to the parking spot in front, where he'd magicked his Jag as soon as Lucy had questioned how he got to her so quickly.

The familiar surroundings that the luxury automobile afforded relaxed Juniper, did away with the sense of being on alert for a pending attack. He hoped it did the same for Luciana. He placed his hand on her shoulder as she made the call to the police, mentally sending messages of safety and well-being. Not that it was his forte, his gift, to soothe and reassure people, but in this moment he could sense the fear that was hidden under the cool façade Lucy tried to project, and he wanted her to feel safe, protected, with him. He wanted her to recognize that he would take care of her.

She explained to the 9-1-1 operator what she'd found when she returned from her trip, gave her address, and sat back to wait. Strangers might have been fooled by her calm demeanor, but not Juniper. Under his fingertips he detected the anxious jumping of her nerves, the quivering of her skin, despite how calm she tried to appear.

She reached out and patted the dashboard. "Got your Jag back, I see," she commented.

"Uh . . . yeah."

"Good for you." She looked at him. "It means a lot to you." It wasn't a question. It was a statement.

He shrugged. "I like it," he said. After he thought about it, he added, "I like driving it."

Lucy nodded her head. "That night you picked me up at the police station, I overheard you and Val. That was cold of her, to break up with you just because your car was repossessed."

Be honest. Don't let the lie rest. "Valentina assumed it had been repossessed."

"But it hadn't been?"

He sighed. "No." He looked out the window. Next was the hard part.

"But you let her believe that it had been?"

He looked her full in the face, trying to judge by her expression what she thought of that.

"Yes," he finally said.

"Wh . . ." She stopped herself and looked away as the answer came to her. "And Val showed just why she was dating you." She looked back at his face, judging if she'd guessed correctly. "She was interested in what you had, where you could take her, instead of in you yourself."

Juniper remained quiet.

"You could have told her that it hadn't been repossessed, but you didn't."

He still didn't say anything.

"Or you could have driven the Jag that evening and still been dating her."

There was still no comment from Juniper.

"You wanted to know what she would do if she thought you didn't have the money to keep a car like this one."

He was saved from commenting by the arrival of the police.

■ ◆ ■

It took the better part of an hour for the police to hear the story, examine the apartment, take pictures, ask questions. Luciana got out of Juniper's car, but she had to lean against the fender for support. The adrenaline was fading, as was her energy.

"Anything missing?" the officer asked .

"Not that I can tell," she answered. "Nothing important, in any case."

Except your peace of mind, your sense of safety, Juniper thought.

"And who are you?" the policeman asked.

"Juniper Penn," he answered. "I'm a friend. I was on the phone with Miss Diez when she got home and saw the door. I arrived just after that."

When Lucy explained about the battered wife and having the abusive husband, Doozy Collins, arrested, the officer gave a disgusted look and shook his head. "Lucky you weren't home at the time."

"I was on a family trip to New York City. I just got back." She looked around. "Where's my luggage?"

"I grabbed it and put it in my car," Juniper said. "I didn't want it misplaced." *And that's probably the only clothing you have left. If he didn't destroy what you had in the apartment, you won't want to wear it again, what with the bad vibes around it.*

"Do you live here with Miss Diez?" the officer asked as the interview drew to a close.

"No, I don't. I live a few blocks away, at the Restoration on Old Main."

The policeman looked impressed. "I've been watching that place. Lots going on over there, and fast too."

"Yes, we've been working hard on it," Juniper replied. "Working day and night, sometimes."

"I believe it." He turned back to Luciana. "You have another place to go? It's not going to be safe here. That Doozy Collins has it in for you, and he's got a gang that helps him do his dirty work."

"I can . . . I can go to my parents," Lucy said. She hung her head.

"I wouldn't tell anyone where you're staying," he said. "Trouble might follow you."

Lucy looked at the officer with troubled eyes. "I wouldn't want my parents hurt. Or my grandmother."

"Your office," the policeman said. "Collins will be checking there as well."

Luciana looked as if she might start crying again. She stood away from the car and turned herself around as if to hide her weakness, wiping her eyes.

"Don't worry, officer," Juniper said. "I'll take care of it. Doozey Collins nor anyone else will get to her."

Chapter Twenty-Three

■ ◆ ■

LUCY'S HEAD WAS leaned back, her eyes closed, when Juniper pulled up in front of the gated pathway, so she didn't see him magick the car already parked there to a spot across the street. When he slammed the door, she roused and looked around.

"I should have asked where you were taking me," she said as he helped her climb out. "Why are we here?"

"This is where you're going to be staying until this little problem is settled," he answered.

"Little problem?" she snorted.

"No more than that," he said. "You'll see."

Wrapping his arm around her shoulders, he guided her to the elaborate iron gate. One touch of his hand and it swung open. "Watch your step," he said. Although the alleyway was smooth, Luciana's footsteps were unsteady, using the last bit of her energy.

They entered a door toward the back of the path, and as they climbed the stairs to the second floor apartment over the rental office, he kept his hand under her elbow, giving her a little added push to get up. "What's the matter?" she asked. "You afraid I'll fall down?"

He grinned. "Yeah, I am."

She thought as she struggled with another step. "Come to think about it, I might. I just might." She shivered. "I'm so cold," she said.

When they reached the second floor, Juniper took her directly into the bedroom and guided her to a comfortably overstuffed chair. "Start getting undressed," he directed. He went into the bathroom and started warm water running into the big clawfoot tub.

"You think I'm dirty?" she called out from the bedroom.

"No, I think you need to get warm," he answered. "and this is the best way to do it."

When he returned to her side, she had managed to remove the jacket she'd been wearing and kick off her shoes. She was slowly unbuttoning her silky blouse, one slow button after another. "Come on. Don't be shy," Juniper urged. "I've seen a naked woman before," he said as he approached her.

"I'll just bet you have," she retorted.

"Come," he said, and helped her stand and start toward the bathroom. "Finish stripping and get in the tub."

He returned to the bedroom and turned down the covers on the sumptuous bed. Picking up the pillow, he punched it a few times and put it back. Gathering her discarded clothing, he put it on the bench that sat at the foot of the bed. Hearing the splash of water, he knew she'd made it into the tub. He settled himself into the easy chair and leaned his head back in contemplation.

Juniper had been in many odd and tenuous situations in his life of globe-trotting, but he'd never before found himself with a beautiful woman in his bath and bed, an ordinary woman at that, who he could not——morally or honorably——touch. A woman who was off-limits. She had come with him, putting herself into his care and protection, and he would not violate her trust in him. He was many things. He was a witch, maybe even strong and talented enough to be considered a warlock. Some would say he was a playboy. But above all else, he was a gentleman. *I will not touch her. I will not in any way imply that she owes me anything——not sexual favors or anything else——for keeping her safe.*

He rose and walked to the bathroom door. She'd fallen asleep in the bathtub, her head propped up at the high end of the old-fashioned vessel. *Just for a minute,* he thought, *I can appreciate the beauty of her smooth skin, of her perfect breasts. I just can't touch.* He stood for a few seconds more before he took a large towel from the stack in the shelves and spread it wide.

"Come on sleeping beauty. Up and out of there before you slip down a bit more and drown."

She awoke with a start, looking confused over finding herself in a strange tub, with a man holding a towel ready for her to step into.

Juniper stood looking down on the street. It had rained, leaving puddles of water reflecting the street lights and the headlights of the occasional car that drove by. All the shops were closed for the night, and there were no pedestrians or suspicious persons out there. No Doozy or his gang keeping watch. Yet.

Luciana slept on. He checked on her often——Why? He didn't know. She was perfectly safe in his bed. Nobody knew of her presence, and even if they did, she was protected in his home—— his territory.

But Juniper was bored. There was nothing on the television that interested him. And he was hungry. He had given no thought to stocking his kitchen when he moved in here. It was much easier just to eat out. At the thought of the meals he'd eaten at

Ophelia's relatives' restaurant, his stomach signaled that it was time to eat once more.

He didn't want to leave. Didn't want to leave Luciana there alone. *What if she wakes up and I'm not here? Would she be frightened? Try to leave, maybe?* He had already placed a protective spell around the flat. No one could enter without his permission. On the other hand, if she woke to find herself alone, she might decide to go someplace else. To her parents' house, or a hotel, or . . . or someplace where Doozy could find her.

He could, if he desired, make it impossible for Lucy to get out, but he didn't want to do that. It would frighten or anger her. Either would be bad, and he didn't know which would be worse. His mind twisted and turned, seeking a solution. He could conjure food, of course, but, in his opinion, conjured food was the nearest thing to imaginary food you could get. Seldom satisfying, it left you hungry soon after consuming it. He could transport food from someplace to his kitchen, if he knew where there was food to be transported. But that was almost like stealing. It was stealing. He could see now that he needed to stock his kitchen with plenty of choices, then he wouldn't be blithering about trying to figure out what to do. When Lucy woke up, she'd be hungry as well, and she certainly needed nourishment after all she'd been through.

After running through every scenario he could think of, he came to the conclusion that there was only one thing he could do: what most young men who couldn't figure out the answer to their problem usually did. He called his mother.

Chapter Twenty-Four

． ◆ ．

LUCIANA WOKE SLOWLY. She stretched, appreciating the smooth texture of the fine cotton sheets. It took about thirty seconds for her mind to catch up with reality. She wasn't in a hotel in New York any more. This was where Juniper had brought her. She sat up and looked around as the memory of the previous day returned.

The image of spray-painted walls and debris-covered floors flashed through her mind briefly until she shut it off. *No. I refuse to let him and what he did take over my thoughts.* She pulled herself back to the here and now. *Juniper lives well,* she thought as she admired the luxurious surroundings, lit by the rays of golden sunshine that streamed in the window. The restrained glow of satin-patinaed wood against the subtle colors in the pattern of the rug gave proof to a sophisticated sense of elegance. The paintings adorning the walls might have come from a museum, or at least a high-end art gallery. *He said he's an interior designer. If he conceives rooms this stylish for a living, I imagine he has lots of customers wanting his services.*

She tossed off the sheets and slid from the tall bed to stand on the floor, feeling momentarily weak. *Food. I need something to eat,* she thought. It had been breakfast the day before since she had eaten. *Is the scent of bacon real or my imagination?*

Her luggage was sitting near a plush sofa across the room. Retrieving her toiletries, she went into the bathroom where she'd soaked away the chill the evening before. Teeth brushed and hair battled into some semblance of order, she dug through the suitcase for less-wrinkled clothing. *I need to go shopping, or retrieve some things from my closet at my parents' home. I'll never wear any of the things I left in the apartment again, even if they aren't ruined.*

Luciana stopped to look out the window. She hadn't had the energy the day before to give much thought to where Juniper was taking her. She remembered passing through an ornate iron gate and up a set of stairs before reaching this room where she now found herself. Looking down upon the passageway, she saw sunlight playing on stone walls, pots of flowers, and chairs that invited visitors to stop and stay. A small lion head spouted water into a waiting basin. *What a perfect place to sit and read a book,* she thought.

Hunger pressed her on. When she opened the stout wooden door, she found a hallway leading to another room and the stairs descending to the lower level. The aroma of bacon and coffee and cinnamon led her on toward the front of the building. The hall ended in an arch, where she stopped and surveyed the area before her. Windows looked out onto tree-tops that filtered the sunlight dappling the welcoming space. Overstuffed couches and chairs offered plenty of seating in front of the big-screen TV, and paintings added color and interest to the room.

"You're up," a woman's voice said, and Luciana turned to her left, where a kitchen filled the near end of the area. "I was beginning to get worried about you. Juniper said you had a hard day yesterday and to let you sleep, but still . . ."

The speaker was a slight figure with curly reddish-blond hair. She was wearing an apron and oven mitts and had just pulled a pan from the oven. She sat it on a folded towel on the counter and slipped the mitts from her hands.

"I'm Juniper's mother, Mimosa Penn, but please call me Mimi. Everyone does. And you're Luciana, right? Luciana Diez? Can I pour you a cup of coffee, Luciana?" She was reaching inside a cabinet for a cup.

"Uh, no, thank you." She'd never given any thought to Juniper having a mother. Or a father, either, for that matter. It caught her by surprise. "I'd take some hot tea, if you have any."

"I don't think . . ." Mimi started opening doors, searching. "Juniper doesn't drink tea, he drinks coffee, so he probably doesn't have any." She searched, without luck, for Luciana's drink of choice. "But I know just where to get some. Alfreda has tea. All kinds of tea."

I wonder who Alfreda is? Another member of Juniper's family? thought Luciana.

"Let me pour you a glass of orange juice. You can be drinking that while I fetch the tea. I'll bet you're hungry. Juniper said you didn't have dinner."

"Yes, thank you. Orange juice would be good."

"It's probably what you need right now, some natural sugar." Mimi opened the refrigerator and took out a carton of juice. As if by magick, she had a glass in her hand and was pouring the juice.

I must be a little out of it. I didn't even see her get a glass out.

"Here, you sip on this while I . . . uh . . . run get the tea."

"I don't want to put you out. I can do without the tea. This will be fine." Luciana took a sip. The juice was sweet and good. She felt herself regaining energy as soon as it reached her stomach.

"It's not trouble, really it isn't," Mimi said. "It won't take a minute. Alfreda's shop is just down the way. I'll be right back." She exited into the hall.

Luciana walked to the front windows and looked out. It was still early. She didn't see anyone on the sidewalk. Shoppers would come later, she was sure. *Maybe I'll get a chance to explore all these new places before I go,* she thought. She noticed a woman approaching the far end of the block. She stopped at a tree, and running her hands over the trunk, she appeared to be talking to someone. Lucy couldn't see anyone else around her. *She must have one of those earpiece phones,* she thought. She smiled. It looked like she was talking to the tree. *Silly thought.*

Going to the side of the room toward the walkway, she looked out a window to see what she'd been observing a few minutes earlier from a different viewpoint. From this window she could see the iron gate she remembered coming through when Juniper brought her here. On the other side, on the sidewalk, a chubby, bald-headed man came out the door of his shop and began sweeping the sidewalk. After a few strokes, he looked around, raised his hand, and suddenly an umbrella opened, hanging from the eave. Going to the other side of the door, he repeated the action. *Now what kind of a gadget does he have to do that?* she wondered. *How does he keep the umbrellas hidden and then pop them out like that?*

When he went back in the shop, Lucy turned and walked toward the sofa. A pillow lay at one end, and a soft blanket was thrown across the back.

"I'm afraid I didn't train my son very well," Mimi said as she came back into the room. "He left his bedclothes there instead of putting them away."

I didn't even hear her come up the stairs. Lucy frowned. "He slept on the sofa last night?"

"Yes. He said it's very comfortable," she said. "I got black tea and green tea. I forgot to ask you which one you like." She held up two small paper bags.

"Black, please. I really hate to put you out. And Juniper. I hate that I took his bed."

"Oh, don't worry about Juniper. He's hardy. It didn't hurt him." She ran water into a kettle and put it on the stove. "And he didn't mind a bit. He's been very upset about the woman who was abused, the one you helped, and he's determined that nothing bad will happen to you." She took a cup and saucer from the cabinet. "He'd never run into that ugly truth before, that some men abuse their wives and girlfriends. Never thought about, I guess. Nothing like that ever happened in our family or circle of friends. Now that evil has slapped him in the face, he doesn't know what to do about it. He can't change the world, after all, as much as he'd like to." She reached into one of the bags, withdrew a teabag, and placed it in the cup. "But my son has never been one to ignore injustice. What he can do is keep you safe, and he's determined to do that." The teakettle screamed. She picked it up and started pouring.

"Sugar?" she asked, looking up. "Milk or cream?"

"Just black, thank you," Luciana answered.

Mimi pushed the cup and saucer toward her. "Sit. Sit and drink your tea while I fix you some breakfast. Eggs? Bacon?"

"Yes, but I could fix it myself." Lucy hated for Juniper's mother to wait on her. She was used to being independent.

"You just sit there. I'm enjoying myself. I like being in the kitchen, and now that Juniper and Ziniyah are grown and gone, I don't have anybody to cook for except myself, except when I have grandchildren visiting."

Mimi busied herself, placing bacon in a skillet. "How do you like your eggs?"

"Scrambled, please." Luciana settled herself onto a stool on the other side of the island and sipped her tea.

"Juniper will be back here sometime," Mimi said. "I think they might have another tenant moving in one of the buildings soon, and he has to meet with each new shop owner and find out exactly what they need their interior to be like. He does all the interiors, you know."

"I don't know much about what he does," Luciana said. "When we first met—when he helped me catch my grandmother's dog—he said he was an interior designer, but we didn't talk about it much."

"He caught a dog? He didn't tell me how you two met. That sounds interesting."

"I had gone by my parents' home to visit with Ya-ya—that's my grandmother—and her little dog got out and ran off. Ya-ya is crazy about Roscoe, claims white dogs keeps witches away, and I was chasing him across the park. I was so scared he would run into the street or disappear entirely, but he ran right up to Juniper and let him pick him up."

"White dogs keep witches away?" Mimi paused in cracking eggs into a bowl to look up at Luciana. "I've never heard of that."

"Well, Ya-ya is from the old country, and she knows all the old-wives tales. You can't tell her that there's not any such thing as witches, so I don't even try.

"Anyway, I tripped when I was chasing Roscoe, and Juniper had to help get both me and Roscoe home."

Mimi frowned as she whipped the eggs into a froth and poured them into a waiting skillet. "He didn't tell me about it, but I imagine it was the day he got disgusted with a couple he was designing for. They couldn't agree on anything. What one liked, the other couldn't stand. Juniper said when he couldn't take it anymore, he went and sat in the park."

"That's the day," Luciana said. "I remember him saying that."

Mimi stirred the eggs in the skillet, then spooned them out onto the plate. "Here you go—eggs, bacon, toast—oh, let me get you some jelly."

"This is wonderful," Luciana said. "Much better than what I usually eat."

"You live alone, I think Juniper said?" placing a jar of orange marmalade on the island. "You don't cook for yourself?"

"Yes, I do live alone," Luciana responded as she forked up a bite of eggs. "And I seldom cook much for myself. I'm always in a rush to get to work."

"And you work at that place that helps people—women?"

"Yes, mostly women and children. Haven Home." She closed her eyes as she took another bite. "This is delicious, Mimi."

"I'm glad you like it," Mimi said. She frowned as she spoke. "And your family doesn't approve of your job?"

"No, they don't. They thought I ought to become a lawyer, like my sister, or something else more ladylike and safe."

"But you didn't want to do that." Mimi wasn't asking, she was stating a truth.

"No, I didn't. I've always felt for people who had problems—real important problems, like not having food to eat or a place to live. I wanted to help. I wanted to be a help. And I think I have been." She finished the plate of food. "That was wonderful, but I know it must be getting late, and I need to get to the office. I've been gone, and there's probably several more problems to solve piled up in my absence." She patted her lips with her napkin. "You cooked, I'll clean up, and then I'll get to work."

Mimi slid off the stool where she'd been perched and grabbed the dirty plate before Luciana could. "Oh no, that's my job too. But I don't think it's a good idea to go to work."

"I need to," Luciana said. "There's always somebody needing something."

"At least you need to talk to Juniper first."

"Talk to Juniper about what first?" a male voice sounded, and he entered from the hallway.

"About going to work," Luciana said.

"No way," Juniper said. "There are people out there looking for you."

Chapter Twenty-Five

■◆■

LUCIANA STARED AT HIM, her mouth hanging open. "Looking for me?" she finally said.

"You didn't think they'd stop with trashing your apartment, did you?" he asked.

"I didn't think about it," she replied.

"Well, you need . . ." he started, then stopped himself and lowered his voice. More softly, he said, "You'll need to be thinking every minute of every day, because Doozy Collins has his buddies looking, and they're determined to find you. He doesn't intend to let this stop with the damage he did to your apartment. He's mad over being in jail, even if he didn't have to go to prison long-term because his victim disappeared. And he's doubly mad because he can't find her. He's already announced to everybody and their brother that you're going to pay."

"Oh, my," Mimi breathed.

"And if he thinks that you're at your office, he and his gang will do to it what they did to your home." He paused, watching her, trying to judge whether or not she believed him, absorbed what he was saying. "Or your parents' home. If you go there, they'll go after your parents." *Of course, the spell of protection I've put on those places will keep them safe, but you don't need to know that.* You need to stay here until I figure out what to do to permanently stop those hoodlums."

Luciana stood, eyes open wide. Finally, she whispered, "So, what do I need to do?" and slid back onto the bar stool, suddenly weak again.

"Let me help you," Juniper said. "Stay here where you'll be safe."

"But . . ." she looked around the room.

"But what?"

"For one thing, I'm putting you out."

"That's nothing," he answered.

"I think I'm going to be going," Mimi said. She pulled off the apron she'd been wearing and placed it on the counter. "You two can work this out, and I need to go see to Ziniyah. She's not feeling well these days."

"Is something wrong with Zin?" Juniper asked.

"Nothing that another six months won't cure," his mother replied.

"Really? I'm going to be an uncle?"

"Well, you're already an uncle," Mimi said. "but you're going to have another niece or nephew."

"Hurray," he said. "I love babies. I love them almost as much as I love little kids and . . ."

"Yes, dear," Mimi said as she kissed him on the cheek. "We all know that." She looked into his eyes, trying to speak in code but get her message over as well. "We need to have a talk, son, about the complications involved here. The ordinary complications. Now take care of this sweet woman, and don't let any harm come to her."

"I won't, Mimi. Believe me, I won't." *And I know the*

problems of a witch and an ordinary as a couple, but my heart is already involved.

"And you," Mimi said to Luciana. "I'm not your mother, so I can't boss you like I can Juniper, but if I were your mom, I'd tell you to mind what he says and stay safe. He knows how to keep you protected." She took Luciana's hands in her own. "Please, my dear." She looked deep into the young woman's eyes as she had Juniper's, trying to both read the thoughts there and send her own.

Luciana sighed. "I will. I'll try my best to stay safe. Really, I will. I don't want to be hurt, and I don't want anyone to be hurt in my behalf."

"Then listen to Juniper. He knows best in this instance. Even if what he tells you sounds . . . odd." She squeezed Luciana's hands. *That's the best I can do,* she thought, *without coming out and saying 'my son is a witch and has the power to protect you'. It's up to him when to say that . . . if ever.*

"Thank you for watching over me, and for cooking my breakfast."

"That was nothing," Mimi said, releasing Luciana and starting toward the exit. "I loved breaking in my son's kitchen. "It may be the only time anything ever gets cooked in it." She paused at the opening into the hall. "Keep me informed, Juniper." She walked out.

"You've just moved in here?" Luciana questioned.

"Yes. A couple of days ago. Now, let's get back to the subject of your safety."

"It's not that I don't want to take precautions, honestly. But putting you out of your own bed, and causing other people more work . . ." She shook her head.

"I have another bed I can go to, if I want," he answered, then thought about what that sounded like. "I have another apartment downtown. The one I lived in before this one. I could go there if I want."

"And I have a job to do, people who depend on me."

"Come," Juniper said and took her by the hand. "Let's sit over here and see what we can figure out." He drew her off the bar stool and toward the couch where he'd slept.

"You could at least let me sleep on the sofa so you could keep your own bed," Luciana said as she picked up the blanket and started folding it.

Or you could let me sleep in bed with you, Juniper thought, taking the cover from her and placing it on the arm of a nearby chair. *But I wouldn't get much sleep if I did, and neither would you.*

"And I'm going to be worrying about the office," she added.

"Can other people not take care of things?" he questioned. "You said some people had come back to work—that's how you were able to take some time off to go to New York."

"Well . . ." she sat down in the chair and started running her fingers over the blanket, clearly thinking of how she could rebut that.

"Are there things you could be doing on the phone?"

She looked up at him, but her thoughts were far away, planning an answer. "Probably."

"You do a lot by phone? Make arrangements, talk to people about things?"

"Yes."

"So you could do that from here?"

Silence.

"Lucy?"

"Maybe." She resumed playing with the blanket fringe.

"You're going to put a hole in my blanket. Then I'll be cold at night." *Then I'd have to sleep with you to stay warm.* He grinned at her, and she jerked her hand away and put it in her lap.

"I'm used to having things . . . work . . . to do. It's not all in the office, either. I go places—do things."

"I'll get you a deck of cards. You can play solitaire."

"I don't like solitaire. I get bored."

"Do you cheat? When you get bored, do you cheat so you can win?" He smiled, trying to pull her into teasing with him.

She didn't answer, but her forehead wrinkled in a frown. "It will be like jail."

He thought about that for a minute. She's right. Even if it keeps her safe, this apartment would be jail for her if she couldn't leave.

Chapter Twenty-Six

■ ◆ ■

"THIS IS A LOVELY SPOT," Luciana said. "Perfect for reading or daydreaming. I've seen it from the windows." She looked up at the apartment above where she'd spent the night.

"You can come down here any time you want," Juniper said. "You'll be safe. Neither Doozy nor his pals can get in. And I'm going to show you how to get around to some other places that will be protected. Now, though, come here to the gate." He motioned to her to come to the ornate barrier. "Try to open it," he said.

Luciana tried lifting the latch, but it wouldn't move. Using her other hand, she tried again, but it wouldn't budge.

Juniper placed his hand on the latch. "Put your hand on top of mine," he instructed, and she followed his order. He put his other hand on top of hers.

"Wow. That felt like electricity running through me." When he removed his hand from hers, she bent her fingers into a fist, then spread them out again. "Like it's been asleep."

"Now open the latch."

As smooth as could be, it slid up and the gate swung open.

"Now how did that work?" she puzzled.

"Magick," he answered.

"No, really. How did it work?"

Juniper just smiled. "As I said, you're perfectly safe in here, behind the gate, but outside . . ."

"I wouldn't be?"

"Not as much. Someone could snatch you. Or shoot you, if they took a mind to do that. It's best you don't venture out onto the sidewalk. But if you should be out there, this enables you to get back in, and nobody could follow you, because the gate wouldn't open for them."

"The magick gate wouldn't open for anyone else?" Her grin showed what she thought about that idea—not much.

"You got it."

"So I'm still in jail, but jail's a bit bigger."

"I'm going to show you how to make it a lot bigger," Juniper said. "Come with me."

She followed him to the door they'd exited earlier. When they stepped into the small vestibule where the staircase led to the second floor, he put his hand on the wall in front of them, running it up and down the smooth stucco. "Did you notice this door when you came in last night? You were awfully tired and probably didn't pay any attention." Suddenly, the stucco looked more like wood.

"I . . . no, I didn't." Luciana hadn't noticed it when they came downstairs, either.

"Put your hand on mine," Juniper said, and when she complied, like at the gate, he placed his on top. The same tingle ran through her.

"Some sort of electric lock," she muttered.

"You figured it out," Juniper said and smiled. He turned a well-worn knob, and the door swung open. "Come in," he said, taking a step into an empty room.

Old. Dusty. Empty. As she looked around, nothing gave her a clue as to what this was meant to be.

"As you can see, nothing occupies this space yet, but more than likely it's going to be the rental office for this block of buildings, and maybe others as well. We——the Pellegrinos and I——are looking at buying more property in this area." He walked toward the front. "Come, let me show you where you are, so you can get your bearings."

They walked through a door, an ordinary door, and were in a room facing the street. A desk and chair, plain and obviously unused, were the only things in the space. Luciana went to the front window and looked out. "Pink. Oh, yes, I remember when you did the front pink. I saw it as I was driving by. I thought it was so unusual——not like any of the other shops in the block."

"That was Sabrina Pellegrino's idea. She has a picture she took of a shop in Italy, and she wanted the same vibe on this one. It's not an exact copy, but it's very similar."

"I love the striped awning, and all the pink flowers in their pots." She turned. "When will you decorate this inside? You aren't going to leave it like it is, are you?"

"No. It'll be up to whoever moves in here to tell me how they want it. The back part can be a small apartment, either for whoever runs this office, or to rent. We'll see how that works out."

"I'm beginning to get an idea of what you do, now," Luciana said. "You come up with unusual interiors to suit whoever is going to be using them."

"You've got it," he said. "Let me show you the next shop," Juniper said as he led the way back into the room they'd first entered, "and how you can get there without going outside."

They went through the same process as on the gate and the door into the empty room to open another dingy door at the rear of the building, and when it swung forward, they were in another room much like the first one—plain and lackluster. Juniper led her across the dusty floor to another door, and when they repeated the process, Luciana found herself looking at books. Stacks of books. Shelves full of books. Baskets with books in them. To the side was an overstuffed chair occupied by a woman curled up with her feet pulled up beside her. A large book was propped up on the arm of the chair, the title, "Practical Magick and How to Use It," displayed. An ornate lamp behind her sent a stream of light over her shoulder. When Luciana and Juniper came through the door beside her, she looked up, stared at the door and smiled broadly, then went back to reading.

"Another wonderful place," Luciana said. Her demeanor suddenly turned sad. "He tore up my books," she said. "Doozy. He tore up the books I had there. Thank heavens my good ones were still at home. I just hadn't brought them to my apartment, and now I'm glad I hadn't. They'd be gone. Destroyed."

"There's all the books you'd ever need or want here, and if there's something you can't find, Eleanor can get it for you. Let me introduce you."

As they were walking up the aisle, they met a tall, regal woman holding an armload of books. "Eleanor," Juniper said. "We were just coming to find you. I'd like you to meet Luciana, otherwise known as Lucy. She's my houseguest for the time being and under my protection. Lucy, this is Eleanor, proprietor of this bookstore."

"I'm so pleased to meet you, Luciana," the woman said. "Juniper has told us all about you. Welcome to my shop."

"And a wonderful place it is," Lucy said. "I love books. I'm happy to make the acquaintance of a fellow reader."

"I know we're going to be friends," Eleanor said, "since we both like books. Any time you want to borrow one, feel free to take it back to Juniper's place with you. You can return it when you're finished reading."

"I'll do that, Eleanor. Thank you."

"Juniper, I may want to talk to you before long about expanding."

"You need more room?"

"I'm thinking about adding a children's section. If I do that, I may need to move my living quarters upstairs over the shop so that I can add more books down here." She nodded her head toward the back of the building. "Or I might want to add a reading room upstairs over the existing shop. I'm thinking about how I want it."

"Let me know, Eleanor, any time. But before I turn the upstairs into a rental unit, please."

"I will, Juniper. Now, if you'll pardon me, I need to put these on the shelf where they belong before I drop them." She smiled and edged by the two of them to continue down the aisle. "Come sit and visit any time, Lucy," she called back to them.

"She seems nice," Luciana commented as they continued toward the front of the store.

"Yes, she is," Juniper replied.

Two large windows framed the entrance onto the sidewalk. Light streamed in, filtered and dappled by the trees that bobbed and rustled in the light breeze. A deep wing-backed chair sat on one side of the door, matched by a counter holding an antique cash register on the other. Juniper paused in front of the chair. "Excuse me," he said to the upside-down child reading there. "Could I bother you to move your chair a bit?"

An unfolding of arms and legs revealed a tousled heap of a girl, long arms and legs going every which way as she swung her feet off the back of the chair. Her big brown eyes opened wide as she asked, "Why? Are you going to open the magick door?

Chapter Twenty-Seven

■◆■

IT BLEW JUNIPER'S MIND. "Magick door?" he sputtered. *How could this kid know anything about magick doors? I just put them in a few hours ago. Who is she anyway?*

"Yeah. Magick door. See?" the girl said. She stood in the seat of the chair, and leaning over the tall back, placed her hand flat on the wall. A faint glow started, and a few seconds later, wood appeared—softly burnished oak, the grain swirling in a pattern as old as the tree it had come from.

"Like the others," Lucy said.

"There's more?" the kid said. "Where?" She turned toward the two adults standing there, and as soon as she removed her hand the pattern faded away, blending back into the wall until nothing was left of the portal.

Juniper would've stopped Luciana from talking if he could, but his brain was frozen with the idea of this strange child discovering the secrets he'd imbedded. She spoke before he could think of what to say to keep her quiet. *I can hardly say 'shut up', can I?*

"There's one back there," Lucy said, pointing toward the back of the store, "and one from the outside to the empty store next door."

"How do you know about this door?" Juniper asked, trying to regain control of the situation.

"I was reading my book," she patted the tome beside her in the chair, "when I looked at the wall; it looked funny—sort of glowy, and . . ."

"Glowy?" Juniper asked. He'd never perceived of the portals being anything that might be described as 'glowy.'

"Yeah. You know, like it could glow if it wanted to. So I stood in the chair to see better, and I put my hand on it—to see what it felt like—and the door got brighter. The more I do it, the better I see it."

"Do you see it?" he asked Luciana.

"I did when she had her hand on it," she said. "Not now."

"Does it looks glowy to you?"

"No."

"But it won't open," the child said. "I tried and tried, but the knob won't turn—not even a smidgen. So I was upside down in the chair so I could keep my eye on it while I was reading, but it didn't do anything else. It just glowed."

"He can open it," Luciana said, pointing her thumb at Juniper. "He puts his hand on it, and I put my hand on his, and he puts his other hand on top, and——shazam——either of us can open the door. It's some kind of electrical thing. I can feel the charge, but I don't understand what's happening. Some sort of new technology they've come up with."

"Will you do that with me?" The little brown face turned up toward Juniper. "Please? So I can open the door?"

He looked back at the girl and frowned. "What's your name?" he asked, ignoring her request.

"Lulu."

"What are you doing here, Lulu?"

"Reading books. I really like books, and Miss Eleanor has lots and lots of good ones."

"I meant, are you here with a grown-up? You didn't come by yourself, did you?"

She slid down to sit in the chair properly. "Yes," she admitted.

"Where's your mother . . . or father or whoever watches over you?" he asked.

"Nobody watches over me," she said, her voice verging on sullen. "And I don't have a father."

"Where's your mother, Lulu?" Luciana asked. "Does she know where you are?'

"She don't care. When she has company, I have to leave and stay gone until her friend goes. She don't ask where I go, and I don't tell." The smile that had adorned her face was now gone, and she looked sad.

Just then, Eleanor returned from the depths of the store. "I see you've met Lulu," she said. "Lulu comes in a couple of times a day to read."

"She tells us that her mother sends her away when she has company," Juniper said.

"Yes. That's what she told me as well." She looked back and forth from Juniper to Luciana with raised eyebrows. "Her mother . . . entertains . . . a lot. Lulu is left to roam the streets. This is a safe place for her to stay."

"Indeed it is," Juniper agreed. "Very safe." He moved closer to Eleanor and spoke with a soft voice. "She's a special child."

"A . . . a special child?" Eleanor repeated. "You mean . . .?"

"She can see the door I . . . made. Even before touching it, she can see it. She calls it the Magick Door."

"Oh my." Eleanor looked at the child, who was now turning the pages of the book in her lap. She looked around, and seeing no one nearby, leaned close to Juniper and whispered, "I've never heard of a parent who was . . . special . . . who treated their child like Lulu is treated."

"Witches keep close tabs on their children," Juniper agreed in a low voice. He stood there, arms crossed, studying the situation.

"She doesn't look like she has pixie blood—doesn't look elfin in any way. . .," she trailed off. "I thought she was an ordinary child."

"Lulu, where do you live?" he asked.

"In the Lyon," she answered.

"The Lion?" he questioned. "Like a big cat?"

"The Lyon Hotel. L-Y-O-N," she spelled out. "We have a room on the second floor."

"We? You and who else?"

"Me and my mother."

He looked at Eleanor with eyebrows raised. She shrugged her shoulders.

Luciana walked closer to them and spoke softly. "The Lyon is a fleabag hotel about three blocks over on Claremont Avenue," she said. "It's a bad place for a child." She glanced toward Lulu. "It's a bad place for anyone."

Lulu had been acting as if she were engrossed in her book, ignoring them, but at this, she spoke up. "It's not such a bad place. Momma keeps it clean, and if I'm there with her, or if I'm by myself, I can watch TV. We have a little-bitty set. Momma says if she can save up the money, she'll buy us a bigger one."

She stopped looking at the book, gazing off into memories. "We used to have a big one, but when we got kicked out of where we were staying, we had to leave it behind. We couldn't carry it, so we left it there."

"Where was that?" Juniper asked.

"The Acme Motel," Lulu answered. She brought her attention back to the present. "But books are better than TV—lots better. Especially the books here at Miss Eleanor's store."

She looked around at the shelves and stacks and piles of reading material available to her. "The Lyon is better than the Acme Motel, too. Quieter. And I can come here when Momma is working and I have to stay away for a while."

"Working?" Juniper murmured, even as he knew he should leave it alone.

"Yes," Lulu said. "She's a business woman. A lady of the evening, even if she does work in the daytime, sometimes. Isn't that a lovely term? Lady of the evening? I don't know exactly what she does, but it sounds glamorous. She says she'll explain it to me when I'm older, but that I'm too young now to understand."

"How old are you, Lulu?" Luciana asked.

"Nine," Lulu answered. "Momma says that's the brink of womanhood, the edge of my flowering. That means . . ."

"I know what it means," Juniper interrupted before she could go any further. This discussion had gone quite far enough for him.

Chapter Twenty-Eight

■◆■

"LET'S OPEN THIS DOOR," Juniper said. "Lulu, stand up, please, so we can move the chair and get to the door."

"Oh boy," she said, standing and pulling on the chair. "I'll bet there's something special in there. I'll bet there's a treasure. Gold and diamonds and money."

Juniper shoved the chair aside and stood staring at Lulu. "Why would you think that there's a room with treasure in it behind the door?"

"Because there's always treasure in secret rooms with magick doors," she answered.

"Who says?" Juniper asked. "Who says that?"

"Books," came the answer. "In books, there's always treasure in secret rooms."

"Well, this isn't a door to a secret room. There's no treasure to be found here."

"Who says?" Lulu shot back. "There might be."

"I say," Juniper said. "I made the door, and I say."

"You made the magick door?" Lulu gaped at him.

"I did."

"What for? Why did you?"

"To get from one place to another. In this case, to get from this bookstore to the tea shop."

"Why not just go out the front door and walk next door?"

Ahh. Now I'm trapped. Got to tell the truth. "Because there are some bad people looking for Luciana. If they find her, they might hurt her. She's safe as long as she's inside, but if they catch her on the sidewalk, they might be able to grab her. So I made the doors so she can go from one shop to another without going out on the sidewalk."

"Oh," Lulu said, staring at Luciana. "That's your name? Luciana?"

"That's me. But you can call me Lucy."

"Luciana is a beautiful name. It sounds like a princess's name. I wish I had a princess name."

"Thank you. I like it too, but some people like to call me a shorter name."

Just then, a short, balding man came in the front door and tried skirting around the chair and the people in the way.

"Pardon me," he said. "I'm looking for books on astrology."

"Down this aisle on the right," Lulu answered before Eleanor could respond.

"Thank you," he said and hurried along.

"So let's open this door and get out of the way of the customers," Juniper said.

"Do you want more tea, Lulu?" Alfreda asked.

"Yes, please."

"What a polite child," the hostess said. "More for you, Luciana?"

"Yes, thank you. This peach tea is delicious. I'd never had it before."

"Yes, peach-ginger is a popular blend. I'll bring a pot of it to the table," Alfreda said, "as well as a pot of chocolate-mint for Lulu." As she started to walk away she remembered the third member of the party. "More tea for you, Juniper? Another flavor, perhaps?"

"No thank you. I still have plenty of this . . . uh . . ."

"Cherry Berry," Alfreda replied. "Not much of a tea drinker, are you?"

"Not much," he muttered as she walked away.

"Jumper? Did she call you Jumper?" Lulu asked. "Is that your name?"

"Juniper is my name. Like a juniper bush."

"I thought she said Jumper," Lulu said.

"That's what my niece and nephew call me," he replied. "Uncle Jumper."

Lulu giggled. "Uncle Jumper. That's funny."

"Do you have any aunts or uncles, Lulu?" Luciana asked.

"No, I don't think so," the child replied. "Momma never told me about any." She took a sip of her tea. "I sure like this tea," she said. "Momma fixes coffee in our room, but not tea. I don't think she likes it."

"Do you come in this shop often, Lulu?" Juniper asked.

"No, not much," she answered.

"She came in once," Alfreda answered as she returned bearing a tray. "I gave her some tea and a cookie." She set the serving vessel on the table. "But she hasn't been back."

"I don't have any money to pay," Lulu explained. "It makes me feel funny for people to give me stuff when I'm supposed to pay. Like I'm poor or something."

The adults looked at each other, aware that this was an acute sensibility for a child.

"Poor?" Juniper voiced. *She realizes that she's poor? Is embarrassed by it?*

Lulu nodded her head but didn't comment further on that subject. Looking down at the liquid in her cup, she said, "This is a beautiful cup. Special."

"Special just for you," Alfreda said. "When I saw you that first time, I knew that was the cup I should use to serve you your tea. It's a gift I have, you know, picking the right cup for the right customer." She looked away before setting the teapots and the plate of cookies off the tray. Juniper could swear she wiped a tear from the corner of her eye. "And I knew that the yellow rose cup was meant for you, Lulu."

"Really? You can tell?" Lulu asked, eyes open wide. "Are you magick, too?"

"Some people say that I am," Alfreda responded. "And I tell you what. Any time you come by and want a cup of tea and a cookie but you don't have money to pay, just tell me. I have lots of work to do around here, and I'll hire you to do it and pay you with tea and cookies."

"Oh, boy," Lulu's enthusiasm almost had her bouncing in her chair. "I'd like that. I like to work—to do things for people."

"We've got a deal, then," Alfreda answered. "I'll be happy to have someone do things for me."

"Not this time, though," Juniper said. "I'm paying this time."

"It's on the house this time, Juniper," Alfreda said.

"No way. A gentleman always pays his way."

"These are delicious cookies, Alfreda," Lucy said, breaking into their good-natured squabble. "Do you make them yourself?"

"I do," she answered. "I wish I could produce more of them, and a variety, but I'm needed to manage the tea. There's not enough time to do everything." She looked at Lulu and smiled. "That's why I offered to hire Lulu here for tea and cookies. She can do little chores for me that take up my time."

"I'll be glad to do that, Miss Alfreda. Anytime you need me." The child looked excited at the prospect.

"Where I work, at the Haven Home office, there are a couple of women who bring us cookies from time to time. Homemade ones that are delicious. I was thinking that you could buy from them. It would be a needed source of income for them, plus a variety for you."

"That's a wonderful idea," Alfreda said. "I can't make a profit if I buy from a commercial bakery, and they're just not the same as home-made, anyway. I'd have to check into the health department's requirements for their kitchen, but they could come here and use my kitchen. It's time that I don't have enough of."

"I'll think about it and make a list of names," Lucy said. "Maybe we can come up with something that would be good for both of you."

When Alfreda walked away, Juniper said, "That's what you do, isn't it? Some of it, at least. You help people by putting opportunities together."

"I hadn't thought about it that way," Luciana answered, "but it's true. Sometimes it's women in trouble—bad trouble. But other times, they just need a little nudge, a chance, an idea that will lead them to something better."

"And a lot of that can be done from right here on Old Main, by telephone."

Luciana tipped her head to one side, thinking. "You're right. At least this one thing I can do here. Maybe there's more. And you're right about something else: a lot of my work is done by telephone. But . . ." she broke off.

"But what?" Juniper asked.

"If I have to meet with people . . ."

"You could meet here in the Cup and Leaf," he answered.

"Alfreda might not like that," she answered. "And what about the safety concern. Would I be putting someone in danger?"

"I admit, I'll have to think about that," he answered.

"What danger?" Lulu asked. "Why are you in danger?"

Luciana shot a meaningful look at Juniper, as if to say this child is too young to hear about men beating up women—not with her mother "entertaining" like she does.

"Lucy works with people who need help, and she had to see that a man was kept in jail until a woman he beat up could get away. Now he's mad at Lucy."

"A woman like my mother?" The fear was evident in her eyes.

"No, dear," Luciana said. "She was his wife."

"His wife?"

"Yes."

"Men are supposed to love their wife, not beat her up."

"I know. I know." Luciana looked into her cup, contemplating the wisdom of a child.

"They're supposed to, but not all of them do," Juniper said.

Thirty minutes later, Juniper and Luciana used the magick doors to make their way back to his apartment. Lulu had informed them it was time for her to go home.

"How do you know it's time?" Juniper asked.

"Because it's about noon," she informed him, checking the cheap watch strapped to her wrist. "Momma puts a red handkerchief in the window if I'm supposed to stay gone. If it's not there, I can go up to our room."

"What if the weather's bad?" Luciana asked. "What do you do then?"

"Well, when we lived at the Acme Motel, I stayed in the office until I could go to our room. The weather's been nice since we moved to the Lyon. I guess I'd stay in the front lobby if she was still working. I'm not supposed to interrupt her." She sounded reluctant to voice that option.

Juniper offered to take her home, but she refused, saying, "Momma said to never, ever get in a car with someone. They might want to kidnap me and hold me for ransom, and Momma doesn't have any money to pay to get me back."

After Lulu left, Lucy said, "I've got to do something about the situation. I'll call Child Protective Services and have her removed. This can't go on. Something terrible could happen to her."

"Hold on, before you do that," Juniper said. "Maybe there's something I can do."

"What could you do?" Luciana asked as they made their way back to Juniper's apartment.

"Find a better place for her to live," he replied, not mentioning that the protective spell he'd placed on the child would prevent the worst from happening.

Chapter Twenty-Nine

■◆■

AS SOON AS THEY reached the bottom of the stairs leading to Juniper's apartment, he excused himself. "I have some important business I have to take care of," he explained. "It shouldn't take long. Why don't you see what's for lunch. If I know Mimi, she left us well prepared. I'll be back shortly."

He got into his Jag, which was parked directly in front of the pathway. As soon as he rounded the corner at the end of the block, the vehicle morphed into a ten-year-old sedan, unnoticeable among the other cars in the neighborhood. It took only a few minutes to find the dilapidated Lyon Hotel. It's rusting sign, only half lit with flickering neon, advertised, "weekly-monthly rates". Lulu stood across the street looking up at the windows of the second floor, where one set of blinds held a red kerchief dangling from the slats.

As Juniper watched the child, the front door to the establishment opened and a man walked out. Pausing on the sidewalk, he looked up and down the walkway, and Juniper noticed that Lulu took a step backwards into the doorway of the pawnshop where she'd secreted herself. The man reached into his jacket pocket and withdrew a package of cigarettes and a book of matches. Lighting up, he tossed the match onto the ground and walked away.

By the time Juniper reached the next block, the red rag had come down from its site. The instant that happened, Lulu came out of her hiding place, crossed the street, and entered the place she called home.

■ ◆ ■

"How long do you think I'll have to stay hidden?" Luciana asked as she picked up the sandwich she'd just constructed.

"I've been thinking about that," Juniper replied. "Doozy will try something else at some point. What, I don't know, but guys like him are impatient. They seldom just give up once their mind is set on something, and I think his mind is set on hurting you."

"You think he'll do more, then? More than just the paint on my door?"

"I do." Juniper pressed down on the tower of meats and cheeses, lettuce and tomato, trying to get it compressed so it would fit into his mouth. It was a minute before he could speak again. "He found out where you lived to do that. He'll try something to find where you've gone. That's why you have to stay out of sight . . . safe."

"I don't understand why I'll be so safe here," Luciana said after thinking about the situation for a while. "Why couldn't he just walk in and grab me?"

"Because everyone on this block will be on alert and protecting you."

"How much can Eleanor and Alfreda do to keep him from hurting me?" she asked.

"More than you think," he said. "More than you know," he muttered as he rummaged in the cabinet. "You'd think Mimi would get cookies," he said, moving packages and cans around.

"Aha! Here they are." He pulled a sack from the back corner. "Chocolate chip. My favorite." He opened it and withdrew two sweets. "Want some?" he asked as he offered it to Lucy.

"Not yet. I'm not through with my sandwich yet." She took another bite. "Okay. You've persuaded me," she said as she wiped her hands with a napkin. "At least you've convinced me enough to stay out of sight for a while until we see what happens."

"Good. It makes it easier if you stay hidden while we watch him to see what he has in mind. Sooner or later, he'll do something to have the cops on him again. With any luck he'll end up in prison for a few years. I just don't want it to be hurting you or your family."

"As long as I can do some business by phone, I won't feel like I'm useless sitting around here. With all that happened yesterday, I let it run out of juice, but I've had it charging since I woke up this morning. I'll see if I can find somebody who could make cookies for Alfreda to sell in the tea shop. That's one thing I might be able to get accomplished from here that would be of help to a couple of people. It would mean income for someone who needs it, and it would benefit Alfreda as well."

"You should never think you're useless," Juniper said. He stood in front of where she perched on the bar stool at the kitchen island. Brushing wisps of her ebony hair away from her face, he looked deep into her gray eyes. "You are loved and needed by many people. Those you help in your job at Haven Home, and by your family." His lips gently brushed hers. "By everyone who knows you."

The second kiss was firmer, stronger. As he turned his head to fit their mouths together in a more satisfactory position, she grasped his elbows, holding him as if she thought he might get away. As the kiss deepened, Juniper's arms slipped around her pulling her closer. Finally, he broke the connection and stepped back.

Wow. Hold on, man. This can never be serious, not between a witch and an ordinary, and I can't . . . shouldn't . . . start something that would have to end. Lucy isn't somebody I want to play with, tease.

He caught her hands in his as he eased away from the embrace.

"I . . .uh . . .," appropriate words escaped him.

"Yeah," she agreed, not knowing what she was agreeing with.

"I better . . ." he stumbled. "I have a client to meet. I better be going."

"Okay," she said, and just stood there, looking at his face, her hands in his.

Finally, he raised one of her hands and kissed her knuckles. Dropping both, he started toward the stairs. At the last minute, he turned and said, "You can go anywhere we went today and be safe. I'll be back later." He didn't look at her as he left. *If I look at her, I might not leave,* he thought.

Juniper spent several hours with Blaze and Clover Hutspeth, the latest people to become shop-owners in the Reconstruction on Old Main,. Two individuals who had been tied to white collar jobs all their lives were at last making the move into what was their life passion: rocks. The kind that were gemstones, or at least had special properties, were what they were going to deal in, but the more they delved into the subject, the more they thought that those stones most people thought of as 'just rocks' had a story to tell as well. "They'll speak to you, if you'll listen," they said. Their acquaintances thought the couple had lost their minds. Although the Hutspeths didn't know it, the other merchants along the block, having heard the latest news about who was going to occupy the small shop near the corner, thought they'd fit right into the mystical community. The newcomers had yet to learn just how special the tenants on this block, including themselves, were.

"You'll lose your life savings," their friends told them, "putting it into a rock shop." But they persisted. The uncertainty was there, however. Did they want a large shop? Or start with a smaller one until they saw if the business was going to succeed or not? Did they want the interior to be light, bright, and cheerful? Or subdued and mysterious? As far as Juniper could tell, neither were mystical in any way. They gave no indication of being witches. As far as he could tell, they did no magick. They couldn't conjure anything. They couldn't transport themselves (or anything else for that matter) to another location, start a fire with their mind, or locate lost people or objects. They were just every day, ordinary people (with the emphasis on ordinary) who knew which stone to wear or keep close by to achieve what you wished to accomplish. And they talked to rocks. Juniper didn't know if the rocks talked back or not.

They were neighbors of Sabrina and Josh Pellegrino, living in an ultra-modern wood and glass home in Apple Crossing, and it was this friendship that led to their throwing over their conventional life-style and becoming shop-owners. Both of them had been born and raised in a hippie community with free-living parents, thus their flower-child names.

"They could have been worse," Clover Hutspeth said. "My sister's name is Starshine, and Blaze has a brother named Dusk." When they became of age they rebelled, as children are apt to do, by becoming straight-laced, suit-wearing, law-abiding traditionalists. Except for rocks.

But now, approaching their forties, they took their savings and invested in the one "New Age" subject they passionately believed in: the power of stones and gems.

"I think we made the right choice," Blaze said to Juniper as they stood in the doorway of the small shop next to the Cup and Leaf. What he meant was "Do you think we made the right choice?"

"I think you'll be happy here," Juniper answered, fully aware that his approval was needed by the uncertain new business owners. "When I get the counters and display cases in, and you fill them with your merchandise, you'll feel settled." He started to add, "I promise," but stopped short of saying that. Some people, he knew, were never settled or happy, and his talent did not lie with seeing the future or reassuring people, but only with magicking interior design to accomplish a desired outcome, be it financial or otherwise.

After receiving sketches and both verbal and written instructions about what the Hutspeths wanted their new shop to look like, he sent them away. "I work better with nobody watching," he said. It wasn't much of a lie. *I'll certainly work better without you watching. I don't know if you could handle seeing me conjure.* He didn't know if they were aware of the mystical natural of the people doing business at the Restoration on Old Main, and he wasn't going to bring up the subject of magick with these newcomers. The fact he was a witch might cause severe anxiety with them. "Come back tomorrow morning. You can tell me then what changes I need to make."

He spent a couple of hours magickally producing a space he hoped would charm both the Hutspeths and their customers. When he left, all it needed were the stones that would fill the displays.

As he strolled along the sidewalk, closely observing the people on both sides of Main Street, greeting many of them, waving at Alfreda as she served people on her small patio, he thought how nice it was that his residence and his work were so close to each other. He enjoyed driving his Jag, but only when he could drive it for that enjoyment, and in a city it could be tricky to transport himself, with or without his car, and not get caught calling attention to his magickal ability. Disappearing from one spot and reappearing in another took a certain talent that Juniper only used when necessary. It might have been fun to do it when he was a teenager, but as an adult he recognized the problems the magick feat might lead to. He preferred to keep life on the easy side.

The gate to the path opened easily for him, and he took a few moments to admire his work. He was pleased with what he'd done with the space. The ornate swirls of iron not only kept the space private, out of reach of passers-by, but framed the peaceful scene as if it were a fine painting. Maybe a few more flowers, he thought. Luciana might have some favorites.

When he entered the deceivingly old door into the vestibule, he heard voices coming from upstairs. Female voices. *Maybe Mimi has come to fix us supper,* he thought, but when he entered the living space, it wasn't Mimi at all.

"Would you looky here," Ophelia said. "Here's the man back from a hard day's work."

Chapter Thirty

■◆■

"OPHELIA!" JUNIPER WAS STUNNED. "I'm surprised to see you here."

"I hope you don't mind that I asked her over," Luciana said. "I've told her what Doozy Collins did to my apartment and explained about staying hidden."

"That's one bad dude," Ophelia said. "Folks are talkin' about him and his posse lookin' to hurt Lucy, here, on account of she got him thrown in jail, and what's worse, she knows where Doozy's wife is and won't tell. You're smart to keep her out of sight, yessir. Smart."

"Ophelia brought my laptop from work, so I have names and phone numbers and such. Maybe I can get a bit of work done and won't be completely out of the loop."

Juniper frowned. "Ophelia, is there any chance you were followed here by Doozy or any of his friends?"

"No, sir. We talked about that——me and Lucy——and I drove another direction, didn't head this way at all." She shook her head. "If anybody was following me, they'd think I was going shopping at that big mall over there north of the river. Then I doubled back to here."

"What about my car?" Luciana said to Juniper. "I didn't think about it before. We left it sitting at my old apartment. I imagine it's destroyed by now. Doozy would never leave it untouched."

"I moved your car to the parking garage of my other apartment, downtown. It's out of sight, and nobody will know it's there." He didn't add that he'd placed a spell of protection on it, so it would be safe in any circumstance.

"You got another apartment?" Ophelia asked him. "Two apartments?"

Juniper had never felt embarrassed by his wealth before, but a tingle of what might be discomfiture ran through him. "I've had one in Excelsior Towers for a couple of years now. What with my mother and sister living here, I wanted a place to stay without imposing on them. And now that I'm working here on Old Main, and we're thinking about buying more properties in the neighborhood, it would be handier to live here." He didn't add that his family owned the high-rise apartment building in the heart of the city, and he didn't pay rent on the luxurious lodgings.

"I should have asked you first, I guess, before telling Ophelia where I was, but I knew she'd be worried about me, and I also knew she wouldn't tell anyone else," Luciana said.

"Be careful when you let her in," Juniper said. "Be aware who's nearby, and don't let them push their way in."

"That fancy gate sure is somethin'," Ophelia said. "Set for Lucy's fingerprints so it'll open for her. When I walked up, I tried to open it, but it wouldn't budge. Then Lucy opened it quick as a wink. Amazing."

"Yeah," Juniper said. "They come up with some tricky ideas these days, don't they?" *You don't know the half of the tricky things I can do*, he thought.

"Did you get your work done today?" Luciana asked. "The new shop? Did you get it moved in?"

"I started," Juniper answered. "They'll be back tomorrow to do a walk-through. I'll make any adjustments they want, and they'll move in."

"I see some interesting places along here," Ophelia said. "What's the new business going in?"

"Jewelry, I think. With semi-precious stones. And maybe the loose stones. At any rate, they're all about stones and rocks and such."

"Semi-precious? What's that?" Ophelia asked.

"Like turquoise, citrine, moonstone, lots more. Not as expensive as diamonds." He didn't add that many people wore or carried gems to add to or boost their powers or to draw things to them, like protection or creativity. An idea like that might be unfamiliar to Ophelia, and it wasn't for Juniper to explain mystical theories to ordinary people. He'd leave that to others.

"Lucy, you know who might like to have a shop here?" the older woman asked. "The Broken China folks."

"You're right," Luciana said. "I'd forgotten that they're looking for a place to have a permanent store." She explained to Juniper. "The Broken China Project is a volunteer group that takes pieces of broken dishes and makes jewelry of them. The money they make goes to help provide a safe place, a haven, for abused women. It's appropriate in that dishes often get broken in abusive situations. We encourage the women to learn from what they go through. To grow in strength and wisdom and be a better woman for it. We tell them that they're still valuable people, with much to offer. Broken dishes don't have to go to waste either. They're turned into beautiful jewelry and the profits help fund Haven House, which is where abused women can go when they need shelter. The Broken China Project sells the product at craft fairs around the area, but they're looking for a permanent spot where buyers can find them all the time."

Luciana turned to Ophelia. "I'm glad you remembered that. Tomorrow I'll get in touch with someone from that organization and let them know where they can find a shop to lease. If," she turned back toward Juniper," you think the Pelegrinos would be interested in having them on the block."

"I think they'd be pleased to have them," Juniper said. "And besides, I'm a partner in this operation as well, and I think it's a good fit. You get in touch with the Broken China people, and I'll talk to the Pellegrinos about it."

He got up and wandered into the kitchen, opening the refrigerator and surveying the contents. "I'll tell you what I wish we had on the block. Someplace to eat."

"Is there anything to cook in there?" Luciana asked, getting up and heading toward the cabinets. "I'm not a good cook, but I can fix something, if we have some ingredients."

"What you need," Ophelia said, "is Uncle Harold and Aunt Rose's place."

"You've got that right," Juniper responded. "But Lucy can't go there without somebody likely reporting back to Doozy."

"No, she can't," Ophelia said. "But I reckon I could go get something from there and bring it back here."

"Without being seen?" Juniper questioned.

"I can call ahead and go to the back door," she explained.

"How 'bout you call ahead so he knows somebody's coming, and I go to the back door?" Juniper said. "No offense, but I'd feel better about my ability to lose anybody who tried to follow."

"That would work," Ophelia agreed.

Chapter Thirty-One

· ◆ ·

"HELLO, LADIES," a masculine voice said.

"Good morning, Juniper," Luciana and Ophelia said together.

"What are you two about this morning?" he asked as he sat down at the table with them. Ophelia and Luciana were sitting at a table in the Cup and Leaf, a tray of cookies between them, delicate china cups in front of them, and a pot of tea waiting.

"We are about sampling cookies," Luciana said.

"Well, then, why, since I'm the premier cookie sampler in the city, was I not included in this endeavor?"

"You've been off doin' your own thing," Ophelia said.

"I'm here now," Juniper said and reached for a cookie.

"I like all of them," Ophelia said.

"Me, too," Luciana agreed. "Do we have to choose?" she asked Alfreda, who was hovering over them.

"Maybe not," the proprietor said. " if I could figure out how to hire both of the ladies."

"Have you tested these out on the customers yet?" Ophelia asked.

"No, not yet. I thought I'd start with Luciana and you, Ophelia, since you're the ones who found these bakers for me."

"But it's your decision to make," Luciana said. "Depending on what you like and how you can work out the job requirements."

Alfreda looked around the room and seeing that all the customers were happy, pulled out a chair and joined the group at the table. "The thing is, anything I serve has to be made in a health department approved kitchen, which——in this case—— means here in my place. I'll buy the ingredients and my baker, whoever I decide on, will bake them here on premises."

"So?" Ophelia said. "Is there a problem with that?"

"No, in fact, it might work out better that way. But . . ."

"But what, Alfreda?" Luciana asked.

"I don't have room in the kitchen for more than one person at a time. And these ladies are very protective of their recipes. Whoever I hire brings their own and doesn't share it. So that narrows it to one person."

"So, I still don't see the problem," Luciana said.

"So, I can only have a couple of these," Alfreda said. "These and these," she said, pointing to a light tan cookie bar and a swirl cookie, "or the chocolate drops and the white ones. These were made by two different ladies, and I can't have two people in the kitchen at the same time."

"Hmm," Ophelia muttered. "Why not . . ."

"Why not what?" Alfreda urged.

"Have one of them bake on Mondays and Wednesdays, and the other on Tuesdays and Thursdays?"

"Do you think they'd do that?" Alfreda asked.

"Never hurts to ask," Luciana said. "They might not want to work every day anyway. These are wives and mothers that have families to take care of. That would give them some extra money and still time to do their own thing."

"Ohhh. Cookies," a new voice said. "I haven't seen that kind before."

"Lulu," Alfreda spoke first. "We haven't seen you for a couple of days. You okay?"

"Yeah . . . I mean, yes, ma'am. Momma hasn't had any jobs to do lately, so I've been stayin' home. She bought me a big box of colors and a color book, and we've been coloring together." She glanced curiously at Ophelia. "You have any chores I can do for you?" she said, looking back and forth between Alfreda and the plate of cookies.

"I'm sure I do, Lulu. You haven't been around doing chores for me lately, so I'm sure there are things you can take care of. Come with me and we'll see."

When they walked away, Luciana explained to Ophelia in a low voice, "Lulu lives a few blocks from here in a fleabag hotel. Her mother, she says, is a 'lady-of-the evening'. Lulu doesn't know what that means."

Ophelia shook her head sadly. "What a shame."

"I know. I wish there was some way to help her. She comes over here when her mother is "working". Luciana used her fingers to make quote marks in the air, "and Alfreda gives her milk and cookies for work. Eleanor, next door at the bookstore, watches over her and lets her read the books in the shop. Lulu seems very smart for her age, and she's polite and well-mannered."

Juniper frowned, but said nothing. *I wonder how I'd go about determining if Lulu's magickal in any way*, he thought as he picked up another cookie. *She could see the portals—the doors—that I put in place. She has something special in her background.*

"If I had more proof that her mother is actually . . . you know . . . I'd call Social Services, but just going by what Lulu says, I don't, and the foster home situation in this county is beyond overwhelmed. I might be shoving Lulu out of the fireplace and into the fire, so to speak."

"My heart breaks for children like that," Ophelia said. "I guess that's why I'm working at Haven Home, instead of some high-powered job, so I can help kids like Lulu and their mamas who get smacked around by their men." She took a sip of tea from her pink-flowered china teacup. Looking off into the distance, she was silent a moment, then drew herself back to the present. "Oh, who am I kidding. I could do the work, but I wouldn't fit into some hoity-toity office. Not me. Not the right clothes. Not the right manners. Not the right . . ."

"What?" Luciana was curious.

"Not the right color."

"I don't think that's true, Ophelia," Luciana said. "Times are changing. Your color no longer affects your job choices. That's the past speaking."

"Hmmph," Ophelia snorted. "That's a rich, white woman speaking. Not everybody accepts a black woman, gives her responsibility, respect . . ." she trailed off. "Not everybody's like you," she finished in a soft voice.

Luciana reached over and put her hand on Ophelia's arm.

"I might even need to hire someone to help with the customers," Alfreda pulled the conversation back to the original subject as she walked up. "I get busy talking about tea and don't cover everything as well as I should. I really need a baker and a waitress . . . or waiter."

"But we worked it out. Miss Alfreda's gonna see if she can hire one lady to work two days a week, and hire the second woman to work opposite days. That way, she can get lots more, different cookies," Lulu informed them. "And I'm gonna keep the front swept off any time it needs it."

"Yes, indeed," Alfreda said. "Lulu is now my employee. She's in charge of keeping the front swept, the napkin holders filled, and the trash carried out."

"Until school starts," Luciana reminded them. "In a few weeks the school year begins."

"I'll still be able to do it," Lulu was quick to tell her. "I'll come by before school and sweep and fill the napkin holders. Right after school I'll check back and do it again." She started toward the front. "I'd better go check now to see there's no leaves or trash. It's important to keep it looking nice," she said as she went out the front door, carrying a broom with her.

"And it's important she has something to eat before she goes to school, and she'll be hungry in the afternoon as well." Alfreda put her hand on her chin as she thought. "Hmm. Maybe I better think about having something more substantial than cookies first thing every day. Scones, maybe. Perhaps one person could come in early and bake scones and cookies, and the other one . . ." she was muttering as she walked away.

"Well, ladies, I'd better get back to work," Ophelia said as she pushed back from the table. She started toward the front door.

"Me too," Juniper said. "I'm meeting with the Broken China Project people to talk about their shop."

"I'm so glad you were able to work out something with them," Luciana said.

"Yes, that spot on the end will be perfect for them," Juniper said. "The Pellegrinos are pleased to be working with them."

"Is that what you're doing today?" Luciana asked.

"After meeting with them, I'm going to look over some more property in the neighborhood we're thinking about buying." He picked up a final cookie and stood up.

"Lucy," Ophelia called out from where she stood by the front door that she'd opened briefly and closed again. "Get out of sight. Hide. Now!"

Chapter Thirty-Two

. ◆ .

JUNIPER SHOT UP from his chair and grabbed Luciana by the arm. It only took seconds to hurry her through the small hallway nearby and into the room with the restroom sign. He turned and placed his hand on the sign with the male and female symbols on it, and the entire thing morphed and blended until there was nothing left but a smooth wall in a dimly lit alcove. His attention stayed on the stranger who'd entered the front door.

He might have been anyone, an easily ignored salesman or shop owner on a break from his job, or a tired shopper coming in for a cup of tea, except for the expression on his face. It was set in an angry countenance, his eyes narrowed and his forehead gathered in folds. His mouth was set in a sneer as he paused in front of Ophelia and said, "Where is she?"

"Where is who?"

"That bitch you work with. The one who has my wife hid from me."

"Obviously not here," Ophelia answered. "And I'd say that your wife probably hid herself from you."

His voice raised another decibel, and he shouted, "I don't give a damn what you say. I want my wife, and I want that bitch you work with."

A group of women sitting around a table at the far side of the room stopping talking and stared at him. An older couple turned and gaped. Juniper took a step out of the alcove where he was partially hidden, but then he saw Alfreda come from behind the counter. *I could zap him before he hurts anyone, but I'll let Alfreda do her thing first.*

"My men have been watching you," the stranger said, "and you come here every day. You and her are tight. She's around here somewhere, if not in this shop then in another one on this block, because this is where you come. I'm going to find her and give her what she deserves for messing in my business. See if I don't." He advanced toward Ophelia, who took a step back.

"See here," Alfreda said. "This is my place of business, and you're not welcome here." She put herself between the man and Ophelia.

"Who gives a shit what you want," he said. "What I want is my wife, and to find her I need the bitch this darkie meets here."

When he uttered the obscenities, there was a sound of indrawn breath from every person in the room.

"Get out!" Alfreda said, pointing her finger toward the door behind him. "Now. Leave!"

It happened so rapidly an observer might not catch every move, but when he grasped Alfreda's wrist in his larger hand, it only took a split second before she punched him in the stomach with her other fist. As he doubled over in agony, she grabbed one of his arms and flipped him completely over. As he looked up at her from his position on the floor, she said, "I asked you nicely to leave. Now I'm telling you to leave and never come back here. Never. And if I get word of you harming Ophelia or Lucy, or if I hear of you using disrespectful language about them, I'll be looking for you. Go it?"

He remained silent, but his silence didn't give the impression that he was conceding. Alfreda used the arm she had doubled behind his back and pulled him to his feet. Observers thought he might have struggled against her hold, but it was obviously useless. The slight figure dragged him through the front door, across the patio, and threw him onto the sidewalk, where he crumpled to the ground. "It'll go worse for you if you ever come back," she yelled as she returned to the waiting group.

The table of women and the elderly couple broke into applause. "I don't allow trash like that here," she said and went back behind the counter. When she noticed Juniper standing quietly, observing, she said, "Thanks, Juniper, for letting me handle it myself."

"I knew you had it under control," he said.

"Yeah, but some men . . ." She shook her head. "Some men have to be all macho and take over. I know you could have . . ."

Juniper just smiled and went back to the alcove where put his hand back on the wall. The door into the restroom reappeared, and he pushed it open. "You can come out now," he said.

Luciana walked tentatively into the room, where it appeared nothing at all had happened. The group of women had their heads close together, talking in low voices, and the elderly couple were staring toward Alfreda, who was bearing a tray with steaming pots of tea.

"Tea's on the house," she said. "I just got this in. It's called Restore and Reset. Appropriate for now, wouldn't you say? Let me know what you think of it."

Lulu was standing by the front door, her eyes open wide. Approaching Luciana, she said, "Boy, you really missed it."

"I did?" Luciana said. "Missed what?"

"Alfreda beat up that man who was looking for some woman who hid his wife from him. And he said bad words—called

Ophelia and the other woman bad names. Alfreda told him to leave and he didn't, so she made him."

Luciana looked at Juniper, who smiled innocently.

"And . . ." Lulu leaned close to them, "look at her ears. Just look at them."

They all turned toward Alfreda, who was pouring tea. Her blonde ringlets were askew, and delicate pointed ears were clearly visible poking through her curls.

"They're pointed," Lulu whispered. "Does that mean she's an elf?"

Chapter Thirty-Three

■ ◆ ■

THE NEXT MORNING, Juniper paused as he was folding the bedding he'd used on the sofa the night before.

"There's something in the air," he said, tilting his head this way and that and closing his eyes.

"Something you smell?" Luciana asked, turning the bacon in the skillet. "Nothing in here is burning."

"No, not like that," he said, resuming stacking the blanket and pillow and putting it on the floor behind the couch. "Just a feeling. Something is brewing. Something bad." He walked to the front window and looked out onto the street. Seeing nothing unusual, he went to the opening overlooking the pathway between his building and Bumbershoots. Nothing looked out of place. All was calm, but it didn't soothe him—the sense of danger was still there, and Juniper knew, as all witches did, to pay attention to his gut.

"I think you ought to stay here today," he said as he put napkins and eating utensils beside the plates Lucy had placed in front of their places at the bar. "Don't go to the Cup and Leaf."

"I was going to meet Ophelia there later," Lucy said, eyebrows raised in question. "She's going to bring some files over that we need to type into the computer. Since I'm sort of side-lined, in a way, I'm getting caught up on some old work that we never seem to get accomplished when I'm in the office. I'm going to type files on my laptop and put them on a thumb drive for her to take back to the office."

"Do me a favor—don't go there. Doozy himself wouldn't go back there because of what Alfreda did—at least I don't think he would, but you're out in the open. Even with people watching out for you, there's still a danger."

Luciana stared at him. He'd never sounded so serious as he did now. "You really think . . . ?" she trailed off.

"Yes, I really think he's going to try again. And he knows you and Ophelia meet at the Cup and Leaf, even if he didn't exactly find you there yesterday."

"But . . . " She poked at her eggs with her fork. "He didn't see me there, so he doesn't know for sure. I was in the restroom the whole time."

"Have Ophelia come here," he said, anticipating that she was going to want to do the work she'd planned even if there was danger lurking around the neighborhood.

"You don't mind her coming here?"

"No. Of course not." He continued eating. "You'll have to let her in the gate, of course," he said. "Like you did before. And you'll have to be careful that nobody's around to muscle their way in when you do it."

"Oh. I hadn't thought about that." Her forehead wrinkled as she studied the problem of safe entry for her friend. A piece of toast and jelly in her hand, she said, "She could call me when she gets downstairs, and I could run down and let her in."

"Yes, that'd be better than you sitting down there in the allée, out in the open, where anybody looking could see you. They'd know for sure, then, that you're here. Let her in and get back inside as quickly as possible."

"Yes, I can do that."

"And tell Ophelia to be extra vigilant. Watch around her for people coming up close. They've already figured out that this is where she comes often, and they assume it's to see you. It's just one more step to start searching the neighborhood for you. If they see her enter the allée, they'll figure out you're close by somewhere. And, of course, you'll be the person opening the gate."

"Uh-huh." Luciana was lost in thought.

A couple of hours later, Ophelia parked her car in front of the vacant shops at the far end of the block. Putting her purse strap over her shoulder and an accordion file under her arm, she locked her car and started down the block. Glancing around, she didn't observe anyone who looked out of place. There were very few people on the sidewalk, probably due to the lowering clouds and occasional sprinkle of rain.

As she passed the shoemaker's shop, thunder sounded, low and far away. *I should've brought my umbrella,* she thought. As she passed the attorneys' office, she looked toward the other end of the block and saw two men get out of a car parked on the other side of the street and start in her direction. One looked like Doozy Collins.

It's my imagination. After yesterday, I'm seeing him everywhere.

But by the time she got to the unmarked shop, the one somebody had told her was a dressmaker, she was sure it was him, Doozy, and another man. If she went to the gate, they'd know her destination. If she turned and went back to her car, they could easily catch up with her. What will they do? Beat me up? Try to get me to tell where Lucy is? Her steps faltered as she debated what to do.

By this time she was in front of the small boutique with umbrellas hanging outside, inside, in the windows, everywhere. A man standing at the door spoke. "Here, Miss Jones. Come in here. Quickly." She paused as her ear and brain made adjustments for his British accent. *How did he know my name? Juniper said to trust the shopkeepers, that they'd watch out for me, but . . .*

Short, bald-headed, dressed rather oddly in a white shirt with no collar and a brightly striped vest, Ophelia was faced with a choice of the known threat presented by Doozy and his cohort or this stranger. She chose the unknown. *Besides,* she thought, *there are two of them and only one of this fellow, and he's shorter than I am. I think that one-on-one I could take him.*

"Follow me," he said as he led the way among the plethora of umbrellas. "Here, right here," he motioned toward a display containing every color, size, and style imaginable. "Stand next to these brollies."

As Ophelia obeyed his order, he reached into a large china stand and pulled out what appeared to be a plain, unornamented umbrella. When he touched a button near the handle, it leapt into a full display of sky blue silk.

"Keep standing right there," he said as he placed her hand around the handgrip, the azure fabric sheltering her head, as if from an interior rain shower. "Hold this steady and don't move. And don't say anything—not a word. Understand? Not a word."

Ophelia nodded, but he'd already turned away from her, and the two men she'd seen approaching were coming in the door.

"Welcome, welcome," the proprietor said in a jolly tone of voice, advancing toward them. "Perfect day for buying a brolly. Or an umbrella, as you Yanks call them. We have all kinds, as you can see. You want two brollies? Or one to share? Alf Birtwhisle, at your service."

"The woman who just came in here—where is she?" one of the men asked. He acted oddly, shuffling and tapping his feet as if he couldn't stand still.

"Woman?" Alf looked around the room.

"Yes, woman," the other man said abruptly, anger showing in his voice. "The one who just walked in here."

"No woman has been in here today. Females, they don't like getting out in weather like this, generally speaking. Gets their clothes wet and plays havoc with the hair-do. 'Course, if she had one of my fine brollies, a woman could stay dry in good style."

"A woman came in here just a minute ago. I saw her . . ."

"Saw her . . ." the other man parroted, dancing and moving around, like a tic he couldn't control.

"She must have entered when I wasn't looking," Alf said. "So where is she?" He turned and looked around his shop.

"That's what I'd like to know," the man said angrily, scrutinizing the surroundings. "Up to no good, likely, if she's hid herself."

But there wasn't any place to hide. No niches, no space behind counters, no place for a person to hide. Apparently no doors to other rooms, either. At least to the ordinary eye.

All three walked around the room—Alf to the area where he'd left Ophelia with the unusual order. "I don't see her anywhere, gents," he called to the searching men. "I don't like to disagree with my customers, but . . ." He shrugged his shoulders. "I don't know where she could've gone. Should you like to leave a message in case she does come in later, I'll be glad to pass it along."

Mumbling and grumbling, Doozy Collins and his companion exited. "Don't know how we could be mistaken about her coming in here," Doozy said as they walked out the front door, and his side-kick agreed. "We saw her go in this shop. Is there another door she could have used?" They stood on the sidewalk, studying the front of the building and talking, one of them bouncing up and down on the balls of his feet.

Birtwhisle walked back to where Ophelia was standing motionless. "Keep standing like that," he said quietly. "in case they decide to pop back in to try to catch you out."

Sure enough, a couple of minutes later, Doozy walked back in and looked all around the room again. Alf busied himself at the check-out desk. "She hasn't shown herself," he said. Doozy looked around as he had before, but remained silent. At that moment, a clap of thunder reverberated throughout the building, and the rain began in earnest.

"This is a day when a man needs a brolly," Alf said, watching the deluge through the front window of his shop.

"Don't mind if I do," Doozy Collins said, and reached for a plain black umbrella propped up handily by the door. He walked out onto the sidewalk and opened the purloined brolly.

"Help yourself," Alf muttered. Suddenly, just as Collins lifted the umbrella over his head, the wind started blowing violently. It picked up the big ebony covering with the man firmly attached to the u-shaped grip and sent it sailing high above the sidewalk.

"Help! Help!" he was heard to say as he was lifted higher and higher. Or it would have been if anyone remained on the sidewalk to hear him, but shoppers had all made a dash for the inside of the nearest door when the rain started. By then he was above the row of shops and on down the way, until the gust quit as quickly as it had started and left a stunned man deposited in a mud-puddle a block away.

"Yes, indeed," Alf said to himself. "Help yourself." He smiled.

Ophelia, standing in the middle of Bumbershoots, was baffled by what had just happened. *Here I am, in plain sight. He should have seen me. What happened? Is it some kind of hypnosis?*

"I think it would be safe to move now," Alf said, "but keep the umbrella at hand, just in case."

Ophelia turned slightly and saw the full-length cheval mirror next to where she'd been standing. When she looked in it, at first she was puzzled, then as she comprehended what she was looking at, her heart jumped. The reflection was of the room around her—umbrellas of varying shapes, sizes, and colors, but she wasn't in it. She was gone. Disappeared. Invisible.

Chapter Thirty-Four

■◆■

"IT JUST ABOUT SCARED ME plum to death," Ophelia said as she was regaling Luciana with her tale of escaping the malicious Doozy Collins by the skin of her teeth. "It reflected the room, but without me in it."

"I wonder how could it do that?" Luciana mused.

"It was the umbrella," Ophelia said, "When I put the umbrella down, I could see myself in the mirror. It was a magic umbrella."

"Come on. There's no such thing as a magic umbrella," Luciana responded.

"Okay, you tell me how I could stand there in that room and those two . . ." she closed her mouth and held her lips tightly together, as if holding in words she didn't want to say aloud, "how Doozy and that other scumbag were right there and couldn't see me in front of them, plain as day. You tell me that." She shook her head. "I don't know which scared me the most, trying to keep from moving while those two searched and me right there, or looking in the mirror and not seeing myself."

"It's a new thing," Juniper said as he entered the room. "New technology. I can't explain it, because I don't know how it works. It's a secret government thing. I think Birtwhisle is testing it out for them." He took a seat in one of the chairs across from where the two women sat on the sofa. "We aren't supposed to talk about it," he cautioned. *It's hard keeping this magickal stuff secret,* he thought. *This is why witches don't hang around with ordinaries much. It's too much work to hold a conversation.*

"So Doozy left and you came over here?" he questioned, getting the subject off magick mirrors.

"Yes," Ophelia said, "but by the back door, so to speak. It had stopped raining by that time Alf took me through his apartment to the door that opened onto the pathway. The rain stopped as quickly as it started. I called Lucy on my cellphone, and she came downstairs and opened the door on her side. Alf looked to be sure Doozy and his buddy weren't anywhere around, maybe looking through the gate, and I hurried across the way and came up here." She looked back and forth between Juniper and Luciana. "Safe and sound." She paused. "For now."

"Yes, for now," Juniper said, lost in thought. He pinched the bridge of his nose and squinted his eyes shut. "We need to keep it that way," he said.

"You got that right," Ophelia agreed. "That Doozy and his crew are serious about getting ahold of me, looks like."

Juniper straightened up in the chair. "You're right. It's obvious that they're looking for you."

"Why me?" Ophelia asked. "What do I have to do with any of this?"

"Two things come to mind. One, they think you might know where Doozy's wife is."

"Well, I do, sort of. I know she's with her auntie in California, but I don't know where that is."

"But if he knew that, he might be able to find her. Second, and probably more important in his crazy mind, is that you know where Luciana is. He's determined that she's going to pay for getting his wife away from him—pay in hurt or maybe even with her own life. And he thinks—he knows—that you can lead him to Lucy."

"But I'm not, doggone it. I'm not. I don't know how, but I've got to keep Lucy safe from that crackpot." She sniffed. "And me. I've got to keep myself safe too."

"I can keep you safe," he said, "but in order to do it, you'll have to do as I say. If you do, I'll be able to take care of you." Juniper studied Ophelia as he talked, trying to judge if she was taking his words seriously.

"So what does that mean?" Luciana asked. "That she'll have to do as you say?"

"I mean she's going to have to go into hiding, just like you are," Juniper said, looking at her with a grim expression.

"Move?" Ophelia said. "Stay someplace else? Not at my apartment?"

"Yes, that's right," Juniper answered. "It won't take much to find out where you live, and then he'll do to your place what he did to Lucy's. Deface it and destroy everything in it."

"Ohhh," both Lucy and Ophelia moaned, and Ophelia buried her face in her hands.

"Or they may be planning on grabbing you and holding you until Lucy gives herself up—like a hostage. They know she'd give up to keep you from being hurt. So you can't stay at your place. You need to move now, today. Before nightfall. I don't think they'll do anything in the broad daylight, but later . . ." He shrugged his shoulders.

"But . . ." Ophelia took a deep breath. "That would be expensive, staying at a hotel." A tear trickled down her cheek. "And I've worked so long and hard to get what I have—my furniture and everything. If they do what they did to Lucy's apartment . . ." She shook her head and used her hand to wipe away the moisture. "I drove by her place, and I saw the mess they made. I need to stay there and protect my belongings."

"That's impossible, Ophelia." Juniper leaned forward, resting his elbows on his knees as he looked earnestly at her, trying to persuade her that not just her belongings, but her safety was in danger. "You have to stay away from your apartment. You can't go back."

"I guess I could stay with Uncle Harold and Aunt Rose, but I wouldn't want to put them in danger as well. And there's other considerations."

"I was thinking you could stay here on Old Main. We have rooms and apartments tucked in everywhere. They couldn't find you here."

"Uhh . . ." Ophelia's gaze darted around the room, avoiding Juniper's scrutiny, "I can't. No, I have to stay at my apartment."

"Why?" Juniper studied her avoiding him. "Why, Ophelia? I can make you comfortable here."

"Because . . .well . . ." she shook her head. "Because of Henry."

Chapter Thirty-Five

■◆■

"I DIDN'T KNOW you were living with someone," Luciana said. "How long has this been going on? And why didn't I know about it? About him?"

"Is he able to protect you if Doozy and his gang come after you?" Juniper asked.

"Not hardly," Ophelia said, looking down and playing with the hem of her shirt.

"Who's Henry?" Lucy asked. "Tell us."

"He . . ." Ophelia paused, folded her arms and looked away, "Henry's my cat."

"Cat?" Luciana said.

"Cat?" Juniper jumped up and paced to the windows overlooking the sidewalk and street. "Cat?" he said again, and walked back to where Ophelia and Luciana sat. "Can't we just put a big bowl of food and water for him? Is there a way so he can go in and out? Maybe a neighbor can watch out for him."

Ophelia shook her head. "No and no. See . . ." she finally looked up at Juniper and Luciana "the landlord doesn't know he's there. If she did, I'd be evicted."

"Oh," Luciana said and leaned back. "Nobody knows about him."

"That's right," Ophelia said. "He was starving, nothing but skin and bones, and I started feeding him. The neighborhood dogs were after him all the time, so I let him in. I have to be there to care for him. There's no one else for him if I'm gone. I have to go home every day."

"As soon as those ruffians find out where you live . . ." Juniper shook his head.

"They'll do to your place what they did to mine," Lucy took up the thought.

"Exactly," Juniper said. "And Henry sure won't be safe then. No telling . . ." He didn't finish the sentences, but they all thought the worst.

"You're just going to have to trust me, Ophelia," Juniper said.

"I do trust you, Juniper," Ophelia answered. "I do, but I don't know how . . ."

He went to a desk against the far wall and brought a pen and piece of paper to her. "Here, write down your address. You said you trust me, so let me go do what I do best."

"What's that?" Lucy asked.

"Take care of things," he answered as he took the paper from Ophelia.

Luciana and Ophelia sat at the dining table at Juniper's apartment. They each had laptops and were typing in information from the paper files Ophelia had brought with her that morning.

"There, I think that's the last one," Luciana said.

"I'm so nervous, I don't know how I got this much work done. But we did good," Ophelia said. "Everything's now in digital form. I'll take the thumb drive back to the office and put the information on the main computer."

"Not until Juniper says it's safe to go back to the office. I don't want you getting hurt."

"Well, I don't want to get hurt," Ophelia responded.

"And I imagine that when it's safe for you to be out and about, it'll be safe for me as well." Luciana closed her laptop and stood up.

"I hadn't thought about it that way, but you're right. I guess we're both in hiding." Her brow was furrowed in thought. "I wonder what Juniper is going to do. It's hard trusting someone else." She rested her elbows on the table and put her chin in her hands. "I've been depending on myself for so long, you know, making all the decisions myself. Doing everything myself." She sighed. "But all this crap with Doozy Collins, it'll get cleared up and we'll be back to normal."

"And we'll be back to work," Luciana said.

"Back to the same-ol' same-ol'," Ophelia said, closing her own laptop. "And when I get back in the office, I'll put all this on the computer there."

"And put the thumb drive in a safe place for back-up," Luciana said.

"Will do," Ophelia agreed as she gathered the papers together and put them back in the accordion file she'd had used to bring them.

"If you stay here, we'll have to think of something else to keep us busy. I can't just sit around doing nothing." Luciana walked to the front windows. "It's stopped raining. The sun's shining now."

"I have to admit," Ophelia said, "I'm nervous about what Juniper's going to do."

"You ought to be more nervous about what Doozy wants to do,"

"I don't know how to fix this thing with Doozy," Ophelia said. "It's going to take him doing something awful to get thrown in jail, or else someone doing something to him, like . . ." She shook her head. "No, no. I'm not going to wish bad things on people, even Doozy Collins. It might bounce back on me."

"Yes, Karma has a way of bouncing back, doesn't it?" Luciana said.

"Yeah, and Doozy's karma is bound to catch up with him one of these days. We just have to be patient."

"But it seems like it's going to go on forever, doesn't it?" Luciana said.

"But it won't," Juniper said as he walked in. "It'll be over someday, and you both need to be safe and comfortable while we wait for that day to come. Ophelia, come see your new apartment."

They went down the stairway to the landing below. The doorway Juniper had magicked to provide a safe passage to the businesses on down the row looked solid and real as he grasped the knob and turned.

The room they entered looked nothing like the space Luciana had seen previously. What used to be a dusty room with peeling paint on the walls was now clean and welcoming. The floors were dark wood, polished to a muted sheen, and the walls were a soft gold. A couch, easy chairs, and tables were placed around the room. There were pictures leaning against the wall, waiting to be hung on the walls.

"My furniture!" Ophelia exclaimed. "How . . .?"

"I've got a good work crew," Juniper said. "I told you we'd get things done and we did."

"I believe it," Luciana said. "How many people did it take to get all this moved in one afternoon?"

"Oh, just a handful of energetic guys," he lied. "I just said 'move everything', and they did. You'll have to arrange everything the way you want it."

"It looks good to me," Ophelia said. "My couch, my chairs—even the toss pillows are just like they were." She walked around the room, touching as she went.

"As you can see, this is the main room for living and cooking," he said, motioning toward a small kitchen in one corner, separated by a bar. "And this way," he walked to a door in the far wall, "is your bedroom, bath, and closet."

"But . . ." Luciana sputtered, "we went through that door to get into the book store, didn't we?"

"Not exactly," Juniper said as he turned the doorknob. *I might have known she'd catch that. She's too sharp to slip things by her.*

"And my bed—my new bed that I just bought last month—it's here," Ophelia exclaimed as she entered the room.

"Of course. I—uh . . . we—moved everything. I mean everything. Go look in the carrier sitting on your bed."

Ophelia rushed to the black box——an odd-looking case with a handle on top——just as a strange sound came from it.

"Henry?" she called as she undid a latch on the end and swung open the door. Out walked a cat—a black cat. Satiny smooth with glowing yellow eyes, he started purring as she picked him up and cuddled him close.

"Oh, thank you, Juniper. I don't know what I would've done if you hadn't brought Henry. I would've been so worried about him. Thank you, thank you."

"You're welcome, Ophelia. Now, let's talk."

"Yes, Juniper. Let's," she said as she sat down on the edge of the bed, holding Henry close. "This place is bigger and nicer than where I was before. I imagine the rent is higher as well. I don't know if I can afford it."

"That's what I want to talk about," Juniper said. "Come with me." He waved his hand, encouraging her to follow him.

He retraced their path into the main room and then toward the front of the building. "This apartment," he said, gesturing all around him, "was planned to be the living quarters for this office," he said as he opened a door. "And the office was planned to be the hub of The Restoration on Old Main. Somehow," he shook his head, "this project has gotten away from us.

"We meant to hire someone to take care of all the records—who rents where for how much and when the rent is due and all that stuff that neither I nor the Pellegrinos want to deal with. Especially since before long we'll have even more property in the Old Town area with shops and apartments."

"So this is meant to be the business office for . . ." Luciana started.

"For what used to be called Pellegrinos Properties, but now that I'm a partner, we need to come up with a new name. For now we're just calling it The Restoration. But someone needs to have a handle on the rental end of things and leave us free to buy and remodel."

"And this apartment, where you moved all my things, goes with the job?"

"That's what we thought would be best. The job, once everything is straightened out, might not take all of someone's time, but it would be handy for the person we hire to live here in order to be close by to show the shops and apartments and to have someone on site if a renter needs something fixed. It's handy and accessible."

Ophelia was walking around the office, touching things. She ran her fingers over the shelves on the back wall, then looked at the dust she'd made marks in. "So when you hire someone, I have to get out. That's what you're saying, isn't it?"

"Not exactly," Juniper said. "We're offering you the job. If you accept, the apartment is yours. You can stay. You and Henry. I've seen you at work. I've seen how you can handle people. You'd be perfect for this job.

"We need somebody who can handle people—different kinds of people—different personalities. That's you. In any case," he continued, "you can stay as long as you need to keep hidden from Doozy and his cronies. Rent free."

"But I like the job I have at Haven Home just fine. I wasn't looking to leave," she said. "And you may need to hire someone before I'm safe from Doozy."

"I understand," Juniper said. "But for now, you need to stay someplace—here or someplace else—where you'll be safe from harm. And this is the perfect place for that. There's no way anybody can get to you here. When Doozey is finally caught doing something to keep him in jail for a long time, you can go back to your old life. You can move back to your old apartment, or someplace else if you want, and go back to your old job. But for now, enjoy these living quarters, free of charge."

"What keeps Doozy and company from doing the same thing here as he did at my apartment?" Luciana asked.

"We have security in place," Juniper said. "You can't see it." *It's magick, and I can't explain that to an ordinary, but neither Doozy nor anyone else can get in or damage a thing on this block.* "But it's there. Trust me, you and everything that's yours is safe within these walls."

"I guess the same thing applies to me," Luciana said. "I'm living for free, but you aren't offering me a job. Shouldn't I be paying rent?"

"No, you shouldn't." Juniper frowned as he spoke. "You're sharing my apartment. I don't pay any rent, or if I do, I pay in work remodeling the shops and apartments. You're welcome to stay with me as long as you want, with or without any danger from Doozy."

"Could I pay my rent now by doing work for you—for the Restoration?" Ophelia asked. "Since I can't go to work, and Lucy and I have done about all we can do from outside the office. I can't answer the Haven Home phone here, or do any of the other things I usually do."

"I was hoping you'd say that," Juniper said, grinning.

Chapter Thirty-Six

. ◆ .

"HOW IN THE WORLD are we going to make any sense of this?" Ophelia asked as they spread the large sheets of paper on the desktop.

"Study and study some more," Luciana said. "The more you look, the more you can see what's what. See here?" She pointed to a section in the middle, "this is the pathway, the allée, whatever you want to call it. And here," she pointed to one end of the drawing, "is the end down there." She waved her hand to the right.

"Yes, I see that," Ophelia said. "Once you start looking close, you can begin to tell which shop is which."

"I think first of all, we need to give each shop or apartment a number—whether it's occupied or not." Luciana said.

"Good idea." Ophelia said, "and have ground floor spaces be in the one-hundreds and second floor spaces in the two-hundreds, like apartment houses do. Are there any three story buildings on this block?"

"I don't know. I've never looked that closely," Luciana said.

There was a tapping noise at the door, and both women froze.

"It's Lulu," Luciana said, and they looked at the brown face, hands surrounding it, peering through the glass in the door.

"Can I come in?" the child shouted, and Ophelia got up to unlock and give her entrance.

"I didn't know there was anything in here. What're you doin'?" she demanded as she walked in.

"Well, Miss Nosy, we're working," Ophelia replied.

"Working at what?" Lulu asked, and bent over the drawing spread out over the desk.

"Working at making a record of all the spaces and who rents what and where," Luciana said.

"I think we can only do so much," Ophelia said, "without taking a look in person. There are a lot of places on this plan that I didn't even know existed. I think I can do better if I've seen the space myself."

"I can help," Lulu said. "I've been just about everywhere."

"Does Juniper know that?" Ophelia asked, frowning at the girl. "Or anyone else?"

Lulu shrugged her shoulders. "I don't know."

Luciana placed her hand on Lulu's back. "Lulu, look at me." The child looked up. "Does anyone know you've been snooping?"

Lulu's glance turned downward. "No, ma'am. Probably not."

"Going into all the businesses is okay, but you aren't supposed to go in other people's homes without their permission. That's rude."

"I didn't, really. Not in homes. I just looked around—learned where doors went and stuff like that. I didn't go in any private places. I promise."

"Okay then," Luciana said.

"Lucy," Ophelia said, "I'm thinkin' she could be a help when we get started working on this."

"You're probably right."

"Juniper changes stuff all the time," Lulu said. "Moves walls and doors. Somethin's one way and changed by the next day. You get used to a hall or steps and next thing you know, their gone."

"How does he do it so quickly?" Luciana asked.

"He's magick," Lulu said. "That's m-a-g-i-c-k. The real thing. Not m-a-g-i-c, the pretend stuff. He's a witch."

Luciana and Ophelia looked at the child, then at each other, their mouths open.

"Lulu," Ophelia finally said, "you shouldn't call people names."

"I'm not," Lulu said. "That's what he is. A witch. You know, someone who can do magick spells and change things, and he might even be . . ." She paused, searching her mind for a word. ". . .a warlock. That's it. He's probably a warlock, 'cause he's so good and can do such hard things."

"Witch? Warlock?" Luciana took a deep breath. "Where did you get such an idea?"

"Well, because of the things he can do. And anyway, just about everyone who lives on this block is magick. Not everybody, but almost."

Ophelia sat down in the chair and held onto the edge of the desk with both hands. "A witch? Oh . . ."

Lulu put her hand on Ophelia's arm. "You don't need to be scared of him, Ophelia. He's not a mean man. He's nice. He won't hurt you. He only hurts bad people."

"Why do you think he's a witch, Lulu? Did somebody tell you he is?" Luciana asked.

"Nobody told me," Lulu spoke firmly. "I figured it out myself. I watch. I listen. I read books in Miss Eleanor's bookstore that tells about witches and what they can do."

"Is Miss Eleanor a witch too?" Luciana asked.

"I don't know. I think she's something magick. Maybe a witch or maybe not. She has Juniper do stuff for her. Move walls and such as that. He made the magick door in her shop. Remember, Lucy? Remember the magick door?"

"Yes . . ." Luciana breathed out, trying to get a handle on her racing thoughts. "The magick door. And the other one, from this empty apartment into the book shop." She looked off into space, recalling other unusual incidents.

"Lulu," Ophelia said. "You said there are more witches here?"

"Well, they might not be witches, exactly."

"Who?" Ophelia asked.

"Mr. Birtwhisle," Lulu said. "I don't know if he's a witch or not, but his umbrellas are magick."

"Magick umbrellas," Ophelia said under her breath.

"He has brollies—that's what he calls them—that can do all sorts of things. They can make it rain, or make it not rain. Move —I think they call it transport—you to another place."

"Make you invisible," Ophelia murmured.

"Yes, that too," Lulu said. "There was a man in his shop the other day, and he was going to steal an umbrella, and when he opened it he couldn't let go, and the wind picked him up, umbrella and all, and carried him away."

"For stealing an umbrella," Luciana said.

"Yes, but I think the man was going to do more bad things, until that stopped him," Lulu said. "Mr. Birtwhisle is nice," she continued. "He moved here from London, England, to be near his son. They had a falling out, and Mr. Birtwhisle thought that if they both lived in the same town, maybe they could make up and be friends again. I hope they can. Mr. Birtwhisle is sad that he's not friends with his son."

"Who is his son?" Luciana asked. "Is it somebody that lives here on this block?"

"No, he lives someplace else. I don't know him."

"Who else, Lulu? Who else is magick?" Ophelia asked.

"You shouldn't encourage her," Luciana cautioned. "There's no such thing."

"Mr. Hawtry," Lulu said. "He makes magick shoes."

"That little short man, the shoemaker? He's a witch?"

"No, he's a troll," Lulu said. "Trolls are good shoemakers."

"And that's magick?" Ophelia asked.

"Well, it is when the shoes do magick things."

"Such as?" Luciana couldn't resist getting into this odd discussion, even if she didn't believe in anything Lulu was telling.

"He makes shoes that make you look beautiful, and ones that help you give a speech, and . . ." she paused, finger on her chin, "whatever you need, I guess."

"And you know this how?" Luciana asked. "He tells you this?"

"He wife tells me," Lulu said. "I help her make ginger cookies and gingerbread. Mr. Hawtry likes ginger cookies and gingerbread, and I help her cook, and she talks to me. And . . ." she looked down at her feet, "he made me shoes, but I don't think they're magick. I haven't noticed anything special about them."

Luciana and Ophelia looked at the child's feet, shod in tan leather short boots, clean and new looking, not ragged like the old worn sneakers she'd worn in the past.

"Maybe the magick is that they stay nice and don't get shabby looking," Luciana said, then could have kicked herself for giving credibility to Lulu's story.

"Yes," Lulu said. "I'll bet that's it." She smiled as she admired the shoes on her feet.

"Are there any more . . . er . . . witches around here?" Ophelia asked. Luciana frowned at her. "Well, I want to know who's who," she said.

"Alfreda is magick," Lulu said, "but she's not a witch. Juniper makes things for her. She's strong—really strong—but she can't conjure, that's the word for it, conjure. She can't conjure up stuff."

"She sure enough threw Doozy Collins out the other day when he came in looking for you," Ophelia told Luciana. "He didn't stand a chance, and her a little bitty thing and him a big man."

"I'm pretty sure she's an elf," Lulu said. "Elves are strong—real strong. Besides, she's got pointy ears."

"You read all that in a book?" Luciana asked.

"Yes," Lulu agreed. "Several books." Just then, Henry strolled into the office and jumped up on the desk. "A cat!" Lulu exclaimed as he leaned against Ophelia.

Chapter Thirty-Seven

■ ◆ ■

"LULU, I'M SURE GLAD we had you to show us around," Luciana said later that day. "I would've never found my way through all the hallways and doors and such."

"Yes, Lulu. Thank you," Ophelia said. "Lucy is right. It was a blessing to have you helping."

"You're welcome," Lulu said as she reached for another slice of cheese to put on her sandwich. "I can show you the other half, when you want. You know, the other end of the block."

"We'll have to figure out how to get there without going out on the sidewalk," Luciana said. "I look out the front windows every chance I get, and I think there are people watching. There always seems to be a guy standing across the street, leaning against a signpost or something, looking up and down the block." She spread mustard on her bread and reached for the package of sliced ham.

"Yes, I think so too," Ophelia agreed. "Doozy and his buddies know we're here——somewhere——and they want to get a hold of us. He sure is determined to get to you." She paused, "or me."

She forked a pickle out of a jar and placed it on her plate.

"When I was hiding in the restroom at the tea shop I could hear what was going on, and according to what he said, he wants you because he thinks you'll tell him where I am," Luciana said. "So he must not have figured out that I'm here too."

"Juniper needs to conjure a way to get from one side of the pathway to the other without being seen," Lulu said. "Maybe a tunnel or a bridge."

Luciana frowned. "I'm not sure about that, Lulu. About him being a witch, and about the magick and all that."

"What's not to believe?" Lulu assembled her sandwich and took a big bite.

"Well . . ." Luciana didn't know how to say that she didn't believe in witches and magick without hurting Lulu's feelings. She hated to step on a child's imagination, but believing in magic and witches and impossible things like that was taking it too far.

"I don't know . . ." Ophelia started speaking, then stopped, thinking. "Did you see how Lulu can see the doors and open them? When we can't?" she finally asked.

"Yes, I saw it." Luciana shook her head but didn't try to explain the phenomenon.

"So tell me again how that works," Ophelia said, looking at Lulu.

"Juniper conjured some doors so Lucy can go from one place to another without going out onto the sidewalk," Lulu explained. "He fixed them so she can see them and open them, but other people can't. But I can."

"How?"

Lulu shrugged as she took another bite. After a moment, she answered, "I don't know, I just can. They look like they're glowing, and when I put my hand on one, it gets brighter, and I can turn the knob and go through."

"And you can too?" Ophelia asked Luciana. "You can see them?"

"Yes. I think Juniper did something so I could see them. He says it's some new technology of some kind."

"It's magick," Lulu said. "Witches can do all kinds of magick. This is a good sandwich." She took another bite. "I like this ham and cheese. Mama only gets baloney, and we have to eat it up in a hurry before it spoils, since we don't have a fridge."

"I never dreamed there was that much space above the shops," Luciana said. "I guess I hadn't thought about it."

"A man who writes books lives in the apartment over the empty store on the corner. He's nice. I talk to him sometimes. The people who have the rock shop live someplace else," Lulu said, "so they don't need the upstairs for an apartment. "And neither do the people who run the *Broken China Jewelry* shop."

"That's an interesting concept, broken china jewelry," Ophelia said. "I'd heard of it before, but I didn't know much about it."

"They contribute the proceeds from sales to the safe house for abused women," Luciana said. "They say that when abuse occurs, often the china gets broken, so it's appropriate that it gets reused for something beautiful, and the profits go to help abused women."

"I doubt it's the china that gets broken in an abuse situation that goes into the jewelry," Ophelia said.

"No, I doubt it as well," Luciana agreed. "But I'm going to talk to my mother about saving the pieces if any of our good china that gets broken. It's a shame to throw anything that pretty in the trash. And now that they have the shop open, I'm going to buy some to wear." She ate a chip. "Now that Lulu has shown us some other ways to get around, maybe I can get to there without going out on the sidewalk."

Ophelia watched Lulu finish the last of her sandwich and

wipe her hands on the paper towel beside her plate. "Lulu, doesn't your mother expect you home for lunch?"

The child scrunched her shoulders and didn't answer.

"Lulu?" Luciana prompted. She leaned over and stared intently at the girl.

Lulu looked around, but finally realizing she was caught, she answered. "My mother isn't home."

"Not home?" Luciana said. "Where is she? When will she be home?"

"Well, she was supposed to be home this morning, but when I checked, she still hadn't come back."

"Come back from where?" Ophelia asked.

"She had to work last night. There was this party she had to go to."

"Party?" Luciana queried. "What kind of party?"

"A real elegant one," Lulu answered. "She had to get all dressed up in a fancy dress, and a big car came and picked her up."

"When?" Luciana asked. "When did it pick her up?"

"Last night. I got all ready for bed, and she tucked me in and kissed me goodnight before she left, but I got up and looked out the window and saw it. It was a limo."

"A limousine?" Ophelia asked.

"Yeah, that. A limousine. A man in a uniform got out and opened the door for her."

"And she's not home yet?" Luciana asked.

"No, not yet. I went over there while you were getting the stuff out for lunch. She wasn't home."

"Where was this party supposed to be?" Ophelia asked.

"In some big hotel downtown," Lulu answered. "They were going to have fancy food to eat and play games and everything. I wish I could have gone," she said mournfully, "but Mama said it was for grownups only."

Luciana and Ophelia exchanged glances before looking back at the innocent sitting beside them. Ophelia stood and started gathering the remains of their lunch. "I wish we could leave here," she said quietly to Luciana. "I'd like to find out more about this party she went to." She went to the refrigerator and put away the remainder of the food.

"I guess I'd better go check and see if she's back yet," Lulu said.

"If she's not, Lulu, then you come back here," Luciana said. "You don't have to stay at home by yourself. You can stay with us."

"Yes, Lulu," Ophelia said. "You come back and stay with us."

"Okay. I will. Bye-bye, Henry." Lulu stroked the purring cat and was smiling as she left by way of the office that was the front entrance to the apartment.

"I don't like this," Luciana said. "I don't like it at all. I wish I could get out of here and check on my own."

"You and me, both," Ophelia agreed.

When Juniper entered by way of the allée, Luciana was wiping the table top. "Why don't you use the dishwasher?" he asked Ophelia, who was washing dishes.

"Dishwasher?" she queried, soap suds dripping from her hands.

"Here," he said, opening the smooth surface next to where she stood.

"Would you look at that!" she exclaimed. "Fancy."

"Nothing but the best for our rental agent."

"I haven't said I was going to take the job."

"No, but you have it for now. Might as well take advantage of the perks."

"He's trying to woo you," Luciana said.

"Is it working?" Juniper asked, smiling.

Chapter Thirty-Eight

■◆■

OPHELIA AND LUCIANA spent their days exploring and improving the records they'd been working on. "Whether I take the job or not," Ophelia said, "this is interesting work. It gives me something to do while I'm keeping out of sight."

"Me, too," Luciana said. "I'd go crazy of boredom, not being able to set foot outside."

They created a file for each location, whether it was a business or apartment, with the name of the occupant, the postal address, and the number they'd assigned it on the plan. They figured it was the easiest way to keep track of who rented where, since tenants seemed to grow and shrink their spots by a whim, leaving it up to Juniper to adjust space accordingly. "We need to keep plenty of white-out handy," Ophelia said.

"This looks right," Ophelia said, looking over the information. "Number 100 is occupied by the Broken China Jewelry Shop. The manager and contact person is Marie Riser. We have her mailing address and her phone number."

"Do we have a back-up person for that spot, in case we can't get in touch with Marie?" Luciana asked.

"We do," Ophelia said, "And we have the amount of rent they pay."

"The apartment above is number 200, and it's vacant."

"This is easy enough so far, but I think it might get confusing when the apartment over a business extends over other businesses." Ophelia frowned as she thought about that type situation.

As days went by, the two women continued to make notes on the plans spread out in the office, identifying the spaces and becoming familiar with who had what space. They used the "magick door" from Ophelia's bedroom to the aisle in the back of the bookstore. When they wanted to go to the Cup and Leaf, they used the one behind the chair at the front of Eleanor's shop where Luciana and Juniper first met Lulu. In this way, they could work their way from their living quarters to the tea shop without showing themselves to whoever might be lurking along the street.

Alfreda assured them it would be safe to enter the Cup and Leaf. "Doozy Collins won't be back," she said. "Not after I threw him out. If he should happen to be so brave, he'll be sorry. Very sorry. And the rest of his pals, the ones who stand around and watch for you, they never come inside." Alfreda gave a lopsided smile. "They've probably heard what happened, and they don't want it happening to them."

Ophelia, who had seen Alfreda in action, believed her.

Lucy and Ophelia explored, becoming familiar with all the nooks and crannies of the completed stage of the restoration, at least from the allée to the corner beyond the tearoom. Juniper stayed gone most of the day, busy with the buildings that he and the Pellegrinos were buying, the ones across the street and on the other side of the alley behind the existing restoration. Some evenings, Luciana cooked dinner for the three of them. Other days, Ophelia was chef. When it was Juniper's turn, he brought in scrumptious dinners from various eating establishments.

Ophelia requested a computer and printer. "That's a necessity for an office these days," she told Juniper. "Got to keep records on the computer, and when the Pellegrinos want to know something, they can access the records without me having to print it out and send it to them. And we probably could use a fax machine, too."

Later that same day, Juniper showed up with her requested items, along with boxes of paper and ink cartridges for the printer. He handed her a catalogue he'd gotten at the office supply store. "Mark everything you want," he said, "and I'll get it for you." The next day when she and Luciana went into the office, a box was sitting on the desk, full of everything marked in the catalogue plus anything else that had caught Juniper's eye.

"Toys for grown-ups!" Ophelia exclaimed.

She and Luciana were going through the items, one by one when voices outside caused them to look at the door. Visible through the glass pane, they could see Doozy Collins and his companion approaching. The door rattled as Doozy tried to open the entry. "What's in here?" they heard him say, and then, cupping his hands around his face to cut outside light, he peered inside. Luciana stood frozen directly in front of the entrance, not three feet away from the man who'd sworn to punish her for having him locked up and spiriting his wife away to an unknown location.

"What's in there, Boss?"

"Nothin'," Doozy said. "An old desk and some broke-down chairs."

Luciana and Ophelia looked at each other, not saying a word.

"Nobody's using it," Doozy said, turning away. Seconds later, the two men walked on down the street.

"What just happened?" Ophelia asked. "How come they didn't see us?"

"I don't know," Luciana answered. "They didn't see us, but they also didn't see all the equipment we have in here, either." She looked around at the expensive desk and chairs, a console table holding the printer, and the shelves, which held various items, including Henry, who was looking at the door with wide, yellow eyes.

"That's spooky," Ophelia said. "How come they didn't see us?"

That evening, when they told Juniper, he brushed it off, saying, "Probably the sun was making such a glare on the glass that he couldn't see inside." Luciana didn't see how that could keep Doozy from seeing anything, but she didn't comment. Before long they were in a conversation about the Pellegrino's latest purchase, the building that stood a street over, and they didn't speak of the incident again.

The next morning at breakfast, Luciana brought up something that had been worrying her. "We haven't seen Lulu in several days now. Her mother left her alone overnight, and when she wasn't back the next morning, Lulu came to us. After lunch, she went back home to see if her mother had returned. When she didn't come back, I assumed her mother was home, but she's never been this long without coming around. I'm getting worried."

"You think maybe they've moved?" Juniper asked. "Got tossed out of the Lyon like happened at the Acme?"

"Maybe. I wish I could get out of here and go check on her," Luciana replied.

"This morning I'm making my rounds of all the tenants. When I get through, I'll see if I can find out anything," Juniper said. "I can go over to the hotel where she and her mother live and ask."

"Thank you," Luciana replied. "That would help me feel better about her."

"We'd appreciate it, Juniper. We really would," Ophelia said.

"If you were what Lulu said you were, it'd be easy," Luciana said.

"What's that?" Juniper asked.

"She said you're a witch."

He was sure his heart skipped a beat. "Huh?" He couldn't think of anything to say to deny it, especially without telling an outright lie.

"Said she read all about witches in those books in Eleanor's shop," Ophelia said.

"And she's decided that's what you are," Luciana said.

"Because you can get so much done around here," Ophelia said. "She's never been close to a man before—someone who gets things accomplished. It's like magick to her."

"Well, if I'm magick, I'll be able to find out something about where she's gone," he said, grateful to be able to get away from the subject he didn't want to talk about.

I'll be able to find out something, I just hope it's not something bad.

Chapter Thirty-Nine

■◆■

JUNIPER STARTED AT the far end of the block of businesses where a space stood waiting for an occupant. Even though it had a protection spell guarding it, he automatically checked the outside for any signs of graffiti, and used his magick to open the front door and walk around inside. Finding everything in order, he left and started toward the next business, the shop occupied by the shoemaker.

As he passed the next entrance, which was the door leading to the stairway ascending to the apartment over the empty storefront, he saw the man who rented the upstairs apartment juggling a sack of groceries while trying to insert a key into the lock.

"Here, Mr. Calloway," Juniper called out, "let me help you with that."

Startled, the man turned with a jerk, and seeing Juniper he smiled. "Ah, young Mister Penn, is it?"

"It is, sir," Juniper said. "Seeing you trying to open the door with your hands full tells me that I need to set up an automatic lock that would open for you—and only you—with the touch of your hand."

"You can do that?" Calloway asked.

"Sure can." And with a few motions it was accomplished. "There now. That will be easier for you."

His eyebrows raised, Calloway tried the new lock. "It works like a charm," he said. "If you can do that," he said, turning to Juniper, "you should do something else helpful."

"And what might that be?" Juniper asked.

"Get a grocery store to move into this empty space. I have to walk several blocks to a bodega to get my supplies. It will soon be winter, which will make it much more difficult. Besides which, it takes me away from my writing."

"That's a good idea, having a grocery store handy," Juniper said. "I'll see what I can do. How's your book coming along?" he asked the novelist.

"Beautifully. This is the perfect spot for privacy and quiet. I'm getting a lot done. People seem to think I'm an old curmudgeon—another Ebenezer Scrooge, if you will—and they don't speak to me—except for that little scamp, Lulu, of course. I don't mind Lulu, though. She gives me inspiration at times I need it. And you insulated my space so completely that I don't hear any outside noises unless I open a window."

"Does she bother you much? I'll tell her to stay away, if she does."

"No, not really. She only approaches me when I'm sitting on this bench," he said as he nodded his bearded chin toward the bench near the closest tree. "She asks questions, and that gets me thinking. If anything, I think my writing has improved because of the questions Lulu asks. Sometimes they're very thought-provoking, existential, even."

"Have you seen her lately?" Juniper asked, not wanting to be drawn into a discussion about the meaning of life. *I'll leave that to Lulu.*

"No, come to think of it, I haven't. Is she missing?"

"Well, maybe not missing. But she hasn't been around as often."

"Hope nothing bad has befallen her," Calloway said, and started up the steps. He stopped and called back. "Thank you, Juniper, for dealing with the lock."

"You're welcome," Juniper said. "If you need anything else, just let me know." He shut the door and tested to see that it locked, then proceeded along the block.

Next was the law office. As usual, the receptionist flirted with him when he came in. "What can I do for you, Juniper?" she asked in a sexy voice, inviting him to make a suggestive retort to her advance.

"Just checking to see that everything is going smoothly here," he replied.

"Smooth as silk," she said, smiling. "Smooth as . . ." She broke off, and leaning forward, she looked up at him, waiting for him to complete the thought. He didn't bite.

"Has Lulu been around here lately?" he asked.

"Lulu?" Her forehead wrinkled as she pulled back from imagining what about her person Juniper might think would be smooth.

An older woman, one of the attorneys, walked in to hear the exchange. "Lulu. The little girl who comes in and empties the wastebaskets for us to earn money," she explained to the clueless receptionist. "No, Juniper, she hasn't been in for a few days. Has something happened to her, do you think?"

"Not that I know of, but she hasn't been around lately, and I'm just checking. Anything you folks need?"

"No, not a thing. Thanks for asking." She placed some papers on the desk and turned to leave. "I hope Lulu shows up."

When Juniper entered the next shop along the way, he was greeted with the scent of leather and freshly baked cookies. "I could find my way to your place from anywhere on the block," he said to the couple sitting at a table in the back of the combination work and show room. "I'd just follow my nose."

"Come, Juniper, and join us," the plump little woman invited. "We have coffee or milk to have with your ginger cookies."

"Milk, please," Juniper said as he pulled up a chair. "It's something I don't keep at home, for some reason."

"You can always get a glass of it here," she said as she slid a plate of cookies closer to him. "Himself likes milk with his cookies as well."

Juniper indulged himself with a bite of cookie and a swallow of milk before getting to the subject of his visit. "Anything I need to do for you folks? Any repairs? Any changes?"

"Lights," the curmudgeon at the table said. "More lights."

"More lights, Mr. Hawtrey?"

"That's what I said, isn't it?"

"Err . . . yes. I added some not long ago. Where do you want more lights?"

"Over my work bench." The troll waved his hand toward a long wooden table where tools were scattered and pieces of leather lay waiting to be transformed into magick shoes or boots.

Juniper stood and walked closer to the counter that Hawtrey had indicated. "That's where I added two," he said. "How about we just make these brighter?"

"That might work," the old man said. "Maybe."

It took one swipe of Juniper's hand to make the existing lamps glow brighter. "There you go, Mr. Hawtrey. Think that will do?"

"I reckon it might." He squinted toward his work area. "Before long there won't be as much sunlight, ya know, and I need plenty of light to get my work done. Then where would you be?"

Juniper refrained from pointing out that he came by every week or two, checking to see if anything more was needed. He stood back and looked around the showroom. The cubicles on all sides of the display area were filled with shoes. Only those persons familiar with the custom shoes knew what made them so special—the magick that allowed the wearer to accomplish tasks far beyond his or her usual abilities.

"And your business," Juniper said, "is it as good as you expected?"

"Could be better," the old man said, pulling on his white beard.

"Business has been good," Mrs. Hawtry said. "Him is always busy making one thing or another. Him's thinking of making bags—handbags and traveling bags and such."

"That sounds like a winner," Juniper said. "I imagine there would be a good market for magickal trappings of that sort." He took a step toward the door, then thought of the other purpose of his visit. "Say, have you seen Lulu lately? You know, the little girl who hangs out around the neighborhood?"

"Not lately, come to think of it," Mrs. Hawtrey said. "She likes to help me make cookies—says she's learning how to do it so she'll be ready when she has a kitchen of her own. Poor tyke. She's as bright as a new penny, and no place to call a home except a hotel room."

"She hasn't been around lately, and we're beginning to think the mother has moved them to someplace else. I just want to be sure she's in a safe place."

"Moved? Maybe so," Mrs. Hawtrey said. "Him made her a pair of shoes—short boots, really. Her old shoes were worn through, so he fixed her up with ones that won't wear out, and they'll always fit, no matter how much she grows. She was real proud of 'em. Course, she didn't know they was special, but as smart as she is, she'll figure it out."

"Yes, she showed them to me," Juniper said. "She's very proud of them. It was kind of Mr. Hawtrey to make them for her."

Mrs. Hawtrey's fingers played with the hem of her apron. "Him can be kind, him can. Or . . ."

Juniper couldn't resist hinting for just a little more information after such a statement. "Or . . .?"

Her voice lowered as she confided. " You know that Doozy feller what's been hanging around lately? And that man what's always two steps behind him?"

"Yes, I know who you're talking about. They've caused a lot of trouble."

"Well, then, that feller——not Doozy——the other one, when they first started coming around the neighborhood he thought he'd pinch him a pair of shoes. Put 'em right on, he did, 'to see what they feel like', he said. The Mister, him knew what was goin' on—knew the feller warn't gonna pay, so he says, 'Here, let me shine the dust offn 'em.' So he took a rag and buffed 'em up right good. And the feller, he says, 'thanks very much for the shoes.'

"The Mister, he says, 'them's right expensive shoes', an' the feller says, 'I'll try 'em out an' if I likes 'em, I'll come back and pay.'" She chuckled at the thought. "He's been fallin' down ever since then. Can't keep his feet still—they keep movin' no matter what—and he can't seem to walk without tripping."

"Looks like he'd figure out it's the shoes," Juniper said, "and pull them off."

"That's part of the magick the Mister put on the shoes when he polished 'em," Mrs. Hawtrey said. "The feller can't pull 'em off. They're on for good, they are, unless he comes back and lets the Mister take em off. Or he could pay for 'em, then he wouldn't fall down no more, and he'd have himself a good a pair of shoes as ever was."

"You think he'll ever do that?" Juniper asked. "Come back and pay?"

"Nah," she said. "Folks like that, they never do figure out why things go wrong for 'em. And for bad folks, like that Doozy and his shadow, things do go wrong. Sooner or later they go very wrong."

Chapter Forty

■ ◆ ■

WHEN JUNIPER LEFT the cobbler's place of business, he stopped at the next shop along the way and looked through the front window. He could have used his magick to enter, but he was too wise a man to do that. He'd heard all about Madame from his sister, Ziniyah, and had no doubt that she was a woman of superlative powers, no matter if she was a witch or some other magkical person. Whether she was in residence at this inconspicuous shop in America or at some other location, perhaps in Europe or another locality around the globe, was beside the point. He hadn't been invited into her space, so it would be rude, even foolish, to enter. Everything looked in order, as it did each time he peered through the glass, and he went on his way.

At Bumbershoots, all was well. Business was booming, Alf Birtwhisle said, and nothing needed changing, nor repaired, nor added. "No more trouble with Doozy Collins or his sidekick?" Juniper asked.

"Not a lick," Alf said. "Not since Doozy stole the umbrella what carried him to the next block and deposited him in that mud puddle. Maybe he can't stand the thought of brollies these days." He snickered at the thought.

"Have you seen Lulu lately?" Juniper asked.

"No, come to think of it, I haven't," Alf said. "And she usually comes by every couple of days to visit with me and talk about my brollies."

Juniper puzzled a moment over that statement, wondering just how much could be discussed about umbrellas, then said, "Well, then, I'll be on my way," and went on up the street. He passed by the rental office, after glancing inside and seeing it empty. Luciana and Ophelia were probably in Ophelia's apartment, pouring over the records they were organizing on the Restoration properties. He hoped Ophelia would stay on in the job of leasing agent. It would be a great help to leave it in her capable hands while he continued with the new remodeling projects. He was glad she was getting well acquainted with the properties on this block before he and the Pellegrinos started adding more to the Restoration in Old Town. Much more would be added before long.

He frowned as he passed the next shop. Dilapidated and abandoned, the space cried out for a remodel—but to what end? He'd already borrowed from the backroom to add Ophelia's bedroom, and he'd appropriated all of the upstairs for his own apartment. He needed to find a business to move into the space that only needed a showroom and a modest area in the backroom.

Next to that was Eleanor's bookstore. She was checking out a customer when he entered. "So happy to have found your shop," the customer was saying. "And I'll tell my reading group about it."

Juniper stood to one side until Eleanor was free, then

approached her. "Everything going smoothly?" he asked. "Anything I need to do for you?"

"Juniper, you are the most attentive landlord I've ever had," she said, "coming by as you do to check on things. Everything is perfect, thank you."

"Haven't decided on the second floor yet?" he asked.

"No, not yet, but I'm pretty sure I'm going to want my apartment up there, and then the space down here on the main floor turned into more sales space."

"When you get ready, just let me know," Juniper said. "Say, has Lulu been around lately?"

"No, she hasn't, and to tell you the truth, I'm getting kind of worried. It's not like her to stay away so long."

"We're thinking her mother might have moved again. I'm going to check on it."

"When you do, let me know," Eleanor said.

The next business was Lulu's favorite, and Juniper knew that if she'd been anywhere on the block it would be here to this shop where she worked for tea and cookies. Lately Alfreda had been substituting a glass of milk for a cup of tea.

"Hiyo, Juniper," Alfeda said when he entered the shop. Business was brisk, with a new waitress buzzing among the tables and a new person behind the counter.

"Hiyo, Alfreda," he responded. "You look busy."

"Always," she said. "Lucy and Ophelia have set me up with some good help, and I'm ready to talk to you about expanding."

"Expanding?" he repeated. "Already?"

"Yes indeed," she said. "I can see that I need more room."

"Where do you plan to make this space?"

"First, although I think the patio has been good so far, fall and winter aren't far off, and then it will be too cold for my customers to sit outside."

"I can see where that would be true," Juniper agreed. "We

still have some warm weather left. Do you want to wait a while before we do away with the outside area?"

"Yes, I think that would be best, but it won't be long before I ask you to convert it to inside space."

"Is that all you want done?"

"No, it's not. I think I want to move my living quarters upstairs over the shop and use the area my bedroom is occupying for more dining space——maybe part of it for a private room of sorts."

"Private room?" Juniper questioned.

"Well, not completely private, maybe closed off by folding doors or something. A place I can use for birthday parties or wedding showers or such. My mind is full of ideas."

"How about I come back in a day or two, when we both have time to sit down and talk——maybe draw some plans. If you have any pictures of what you want, that would be great."

"That would be perfect, Juniper. We can do that."

"And leave the patio part until winter sets in?"

"At least until it turns colder."

"You know we'll have to do the er . . . transformation at night when you're closed?"

"I hadn't thought about it, but yes, I see that," Alfreda said. She clapped her hands. "I'm so excited. I'm loving my business and all the people I'm meeting. I can't wait to see it grow."

Juniper started to leave, then thought of his other chore. "Say, Alfreda, have you seen Lulu lately?"

"No, Juniper, I haven't." The smile left her face and she turned solemn. "I've been wondering about her, whether she's getting enough to eat, and if she's safe. Has anyone on the block seen her?"

"No, not so far. I have a couple of places yet to check."

As he left the tea room, his worries about the young girl who was a favorite of everyone in the neighborhood grew even more, and he determined to find her before the day was out.

Chapter Forty-One

■ ◆ ■

WHEN JUNIPER ENTERED the rock shop, he marveled at the changes in the appearance of the couple behind the long glass cabinet. The last he'd seen him, Blaze Hutspeth had been wearing a three-piece suit, white shirt and tie, and a Chamber of Commerce pin had adorned his lapel. Now, only days later, a makeover had taken place. His graying hair, which had been combed into submission when Juniper had seen him previously, was now in curls and on its way to touching the collar of his much worn sweater. His mustache, formerly a compact line of salt and pepper had grown to luxurious density.

"I'll be with you in a minute, Juniper," he called out from where he was helping a young couple pick out some stones. "Citrine for creativity," he was saying. "Perhaps a ring or a pendant to wear on a chain. And you might want a loose citrine stone to keep on your desk." The three of them walked farther back, to where a basket of stones was displayed.

"Good day, Juniper," said the woman who approached him.

Sunny Hutspeth was so changed, Juniper almost mistook her for a customer. Gone was the executive in a navy suit with her hair pulled back into a tidy bun. The woman in front of him now was the very picture of a free spirit. Her long hair reached almost to her waist and was unencumbered by any restraint. Instead of solemn business clothing, her skirt——a patchwork of brightly colored fabrics——brushed the tops of her sandal-clad feet.

"Hello there, Sunny," he answered. "I thought I'd check and see if there was anything you need me to do—any changes to be made."

"I don't think so, Juniper," she said. "Everything is just great —in harmony, you might say, with the universe."

The young couple brushed by them as they left the shop, and Blaze approached, hand extended. "Good to see you, Juniper." His handshake was exuberant. "So happy to be here."

"Glad to hear it," Juniper said. "We're happy to have you here."

"Best move we ever made. Business is picking up every day. We thought it might be slow at the beginning, but it's surprising how busy it is."

"And we haven't even done any advertising yet," Sunny said. "We're busier than we expected; it must be . . ."

"Customers spreading the word," Blaze said.

"And we sound like we know what we're talking about, explaining the qualities of the different stones," Sunny added. "So they send us other people who are interested."

"Anything I need to do for you?" Juniper asked.

"Not that I can think of," Blaze said. "Honey, you need any changes?" he asked his wife.

She shook her head. "No, not a one," she replied. "But thank you for checking with us."

"If you need me, you can leave word at the rental office down the block."

"That pink building?" Sunny asked.

"That's the one," Juniper answered.

"It looks like something you'd see in France or Italy," Blaze said.

"That's the idea," Juniper said. "Say, there's a young girl who hangs around the neighborhood. Have you seen her in the last few days?"

"You mean Lulu?" Sunny asked.

"Yes, Lulu. You know her?"

"She came in and introduced herself," Sunny said. "She looked at everything and asked a million questions."

"That's Lulu," Juniper responded. "She's interested in everything."

"You'll probably think I'm weird or something . . ." Blaze started.

Juniper started to say, "everyone on this block is weird. Why be different?" but he stayed silent.

". . . but sometimes I get these feelings about people."

"Feelings?" Juniper said. "About Lulu?"

"Well, in this case, yes."

"What kind of feelings?"

"Like she's going to be in danger. Maybe already has been by now," Blaze continued. He rubbed the back of his neck as he looked at the floor. "I don't know . . ."

"I know folks think we're crazy," Sunny said, "talking like that, but . . ."

"I thought maybe you'd understand," Blaze took up the thought.

"He's pretty accurate with this, this gift, or whatever it is," Sunny said. "When he thinks something is going to happen, it usually does."

"And you think something is going to happen to Lulu?" Juniper was impressed. There was more to this couple than he first thought.

"Something . . . I don't know what," Blaze said. "I made her an amulet for protection. People pooh-pooh the idea, but . . ."

Sunny took up his thought, "He didn't tell her it was for her protection—just gave it to her."

"*Tried* to give it to her," Blaze corrected. "She said she couldn't take anything . . ."

"Without paying for it," Sunny finished.

"But I thought she needed to have it on her person," Blaze said. "And I said she could work for it."

"So I gave her some paper towels and the glass cleaner and . . ."

"She polished the fronts of all the display cabinets," Blaze finished his wife's sentence.

"I put the amulet on her," Sunny said, "and told her to keep it on all the time."

"Whatever's coming her way . . ." Blaze started.

"May the spirits guide and protect her through it," Sunny finished.

Chapter Forty-Two

. ◆ .

WHEN JUNIPER LEFT the Hutspeth's shop, his usual calm demeanor was shot all to hell. His normal outlook was cool and collected. No matter what the circumstances around him, he always appeared to be in charge. But that had been ebbing away and now it was about all gone. He stood on the sidewalk taking deep breaths to regain his composure.

Not that anyone observing him would have any clue about the inner disorder he was experiencing. As he stood there looking up and down the block he performed an inner check of his emotions. *Why do I feel so . . . what? Upset? Worried? Aware? That's it—aware. Whatever the word for it is, this is new, and I don't like it. Don't like it at all. This is not my usual state of being.*

It had all started with the sense of danger, or maybe even doom, that had hung about him for some time now, growing stronger each day, that kept Juniper antsy. He had credited that to the constant presence of Doozy Collins and his watchful crew, but surely that wasn't the entire cause of his discomfiture. After all, if push came to shove, he could banish the whole troop of them to the other side of the earth where neither he nor Luciana nor Ophelia would ever see or be bothered with them again. Although he was trying to deal with the thugs in a manner in which the ordinary world wouldn't notice that magick was involved, in truth it wasn't strictly necessary, at least for safety's sake.

Part of his disquiet was his growing infatuation with Luciana. He'd always proclaimed he would never fall in love with an ordinary, and here he was, right where he swore he would never be. He'd denied it to himself for some time now, but it wasn't working. So what was he going to do about it? He couldn't stop seeing her—not while protecting her life. Besides, he didn't want to give her up. He wanted . . . well, he wanted what he couldn't have. He wanted her in his life permanently. He wanted to forget that she was ordinary and he was magickal. He wanted all the problems that came along with such a match to go away. He wanted to tell her what he was—what he had the power and talent to do. And he wanted her to never find out. He wanted her to love him as he loved her—not for what he could do or conjure or have, but because he was a man who loved her, who would do anything for her. But none of that could happen. He was a witch, a powerful witch. As was his whole family. And any children they would have would likely have special powers as well. How could he tell Luciana all that without losing her? She wasn't the type who would want to be with him to take advantage of his mystical power, she was more likely to reject him because of it.

Then there was Lulu, who had figured out all on her own what he was. A waif who needed help and protection. Was he the one to do that? Who else was there to help her? Was she special, not ordinary? How could that be? Juniper couldn't turn away from this child of the streets. She was in need of a good home and a nurturing environment, but who said Juniper had do anything about it? His conscience, that's who. And there was this smothering feeling, brought to weigh on him like a load of bricks, by what Blaze Hutspeth had said. Blaze, amazingly enough, had some sort of talent of his own, and he was worried about Lulu as well. Worried enough to give her an amulet and warn her to keep it on. But Juniper, with his greater gift, knew that an amulet probably wasn't enough to protect the child from what might be coming her way. But what, indeed, was coming? And what could he, Juniper, do about it?

After standing on the sidewalk, studying the changing patterns of the sunlight on the leaves as all the thoughts tumbled around in his head, Juniper went into the last shop on the block, the corner store that sold pendants made from broken china.

"Good morning," he greeted the two women behind the counter. Under glass and hanging on displays were necklaces in many colors and sizes. Shards of china in stripes and solids, abstract designs and delicate flowers, edged in gold or silver, hanging from silver or gold chains, they were reminders of broken promises and broken relationships—and much worse things. There were plenty for the shopper to browse through, and reasonably priced enough for the buyer to pick out more than one without feeling guilty, especially since the proceeds went to shelter the women who suffered broken lives.

"Good morning, Mr. Penn," the older of the two spoke.

"I'm just checking to see if everything is in order," Juniper said.

"Perfectly in order. Business is better than I expected, considering we've been open such a short while. I think all the business people on the block have come in and bought from us."

"I think you'll do well here," Juniper said. "Anything need fixing or adjusting?" he asked. Although he couldn't do it in the presence of these ordinary people, he could come back after hours to make any changes they requested.

"No, nothing. We couldn't ask for a better shop."

I've asked at every other business, I might as well ask here.

"There's a little girl who hangs around the neighborhood. An African-American child . . ."

"You mean Lulu?"

"Yes, Lulu. Has she been in lately?"

"No, she hasn't, and I thought she'd be back by now. She picked out a necklace she wants, and she's paying it out." She opened a drawer underneath the cash register and took out a small, white paper bag with "Lulu" written it. She tipped it and a tissue wrapped bundle slid out. "She said this is like the tea cup that she uses at the Cup and Leaf tea shop." Unwrapping the small gold-framed shard, she showed Juniper the delicate yellow china rose that Lulu had chosen. "She comes in and pays fifty cents or a dollar on it. We don't usually let people put items back like that, but Lulu is a special little girl. I couldn't resist her."

"Yes, she is," Juniper said. "You hold on to that for her. She'll be back." *If I have anything to say about it, she will.*

Chapter Forty-Three

■◆■

THE AROMA of simmering spices and pungent flavors drew Juniper up the stairs to his apartment. Approaching Luciana as she stirred the contents of a large pot on the range, he put his arms around her and pulled her against him so he could reach the back of her neck with his lips. Cooperating, she leaned back into his embrace.

"Mmm. Something smells good," he said.

"Mimi came by and left groceries. I decided to make soup." She put her head on his shoulder and closed her eyes.

"I wasn't talking about what's on the stove. I was talking about you."

"Oh?" Releasing her hold on the long-handled wooden spoon, she started turning in his arms.

His hands on her waist helped her turn. When she was fully facing him, his lips met hers. His hands ran up and down her back as he settled her more fully into his embrace and the kiss moved from hot to hotter.

"Should I come back later?" Ophelia's voice asked from the doorway.

"Yes," Juniper said.

"No, Ophelia. Come on in," Luciana said, pulling back. "Lunch is almost ready."

"Later," Juniper whispered and gave her a quick kiss.

"Actually," he said as he turned toward Ophelia, "I need to talk to you both. It's important. It's about Lulu."

"Did you find her?" Luciana asked.

"Is she okay?" Ophelia questioned.

"I didn't exactly find her, but I found out *about* her," he said. "Come sit and we'll talk about it." He pulled a chair away from the round dining table. "If we'd been watching the news on television or reading the newspapers, we might have figured it out. The desk clerk at the Lyon Hotel told me all about what went down."

Luciana and Ophelia looked at him questioningly as they sat down.

"You know the party Lulu was talking about her mother going to? The big shindig that she dressed up for and the limo picked her up? Lulu kept checking, but her mother didn't come home?"

"Yes," both women answered.

"When Lulu went to check to see if her mother was home, and then she didn't come back, we assumed her mother had returned. She didn't. There was a police raid at one of the high-end hotels downtown. They arrested thirty-some people—many of them very important and well-known."

In fact, it had been at the same hotel where he and Valentina had dined, but he wasn't going to mention that. The hotel where Luciana's sister had wanted to spend the night with him in a room that cost $500 a night. He wondered if Val knew about the raid.

"Arrested? In a high-class hotel? For what?" Ophelia asked.

"They were having what is referred to as a 'toga party'."

"What in the world is a toga party?" Luciana asked. "I've never heard that expression."

"It's when the guests aren't wearing any clothing except sheets. They rent the whole floor of the hotel, and play various games to learn who goes to which room and with who. You might know it better by the more commonly known term—an orgy."

"Orgy? Like . . ." Luciana's eyebrows were raised as high as they would go.

"A sex party," Juniper explained. "With a lot of other things going on as well."

"Other things?" Ophelia asked. "Isn't that enough?"

"Like drugs and gambling."

"Oh my," she breathed.

"And Lulu's mother was involved in this," Luciana stated.

"Yes. That's why she didn't come home the next morning. She was in jail."

"What happened to Lulu? Why didn't she come back here?" Luciana said.

"Child protective services came and got her. She's somewhere in the system, and I don't know how to find her." *All the power I have, all the magick I can do, and I can't find one small girl. Some witch I am.*

Luciana stood and walked over to the bar that divided the kitchen from the rest of the room and picked up her phone. "I'll bet I can," she said. "Now we're in *my* area of expertise."

"If anybody can find Lulu now that she's in the system, Lucy's the person," Ophelia said as she rose and went into the kitchen to fetch a bowl of the fragrant soup and some crackers.

Juniper's tension eased just a little. If Ophelia had that much faith in Luciana, then he'd trust she knew what she was talking about. He got up, fixed himself a bowl of the steaming vegetable-beef soup, and returned to sit across the table to listen as Luciana looked through her list of contacts and touched her finger to the screen.

"Extension 354, please." Luciana said, nervously tapping a pencil on a pad of paper on the table in front of her. "Marcie? Hey, girl! This is Lucy Diez. I haven't talked to you in a while. How are you doing?" She listened and doodled. "A grandmother? You? You must be kidding! Really? She's still a little girl herself, isn't she? Twenty-two? You're kidding me. She grew up while I wasn't watching." She listened some more.

"Marcie, here's why I'm calling. I'm looking for someone in the CPS system, and I thought you could help me." Pause. "A little girl, about nine years old. African-American. First name is Lulu. Her mother was arrested in some sort of big kerfuffle at one of the hotels last weekend, and I'm trying to find the child." Pause. "No, I don't know the last name of the child or the mother. That's my problem."

Luciana listened. "Yeah, I know that I'm out of the loop. I've been busy with other matters and hadn't heard about it—you know how it goes." Pause. "Secret? They're keeping it hush-hush? Why?"

Pause. "Ken Jamison? Over at DHS? Yes, I've met him a few times. You know that Haven Home doesn't get involved with anyone as high-up as Ken on many cases. Usually we just work with local and county people." Pause. "Okay, I'll check with him. If he can't help, maybe he can point me toward somebody who can." Pause. "Thanks, Marcie. Be sure and send me an announcement when that grandbaby gets here. Do you know yet if it's going to be a boy or a girl?" Pause. "Okay. Thanks again."

She touched her phone to end the call and started scrolling through her contact list. Finally coming to what she was looking for, she pressed an icon on the phone surface and put it back to her ear.

"Ken Jamison, please." Pause. "Luciana Diez."

As she waited, Juniper thought about the way she changed names from Luciana to Lucy and back to Luciana. Evidently it varied according to whom she was speaking with. She was Lucy to closer acquaintances, but announced herself to a gatekeeper as Luciana. Did that mean something? He wondered if she preferred one name over the other.

"Hi, Ken," she said as she took up the conversation again. "Lucy Diez. Remember me? From Haven Home?" Pause. "Marcie Fulton over at CPS thought I needed to speak to you about a kid I'm trying to find. Her mother was picked up in that big raid last weekend." Pause. "Yes, that one."

"No, nothing like that. We don't deal with the rich and famous. They can afford their own lawyers. They don't need the likes of us." She chuckled, but it sounded to Juniper like she had to force the laugh. "No, this doesn't involve anyone who's politically connected, is a TV personality or anyone else you might have heard of. She's just an ordinary, low-rent prostitute who got caught up in the sting, and I'm trying to find her kid."

"I'd appreciate any help you can give me on this." Longer pause. "This is strictly off-the-record, Ken. And there's absolutely no connection between the child I'm looking for and anybody——famous or not——whose name made or will make the news. Do you have a list of everyone who was hauled in? Can you check the names of the women who were charged with prostitution and see if CPS opened a case on a child connected with any of them" Pause. "Okay. Thanks. But I'll just hold while you look."

Luciana held the cellphone against her chest, hands wrapped around it. "He's going to check the list of people—women— who were charged, and see if they have a file on a child belonging to one. If I were to wait for him to call me back—— like he wanted me to do——he'd get busy and I might never hear from him again." She put the phone back to her ear and listened for her source to return. She continued drawing circles and squares on the pad of paper. Time stretched out until Juniper thought they must be at a dead end. At last, Luciana sat up straight in her chair, alert.

"Parish? P-A-R-I-S-H. Right. I've got it." She listened, then said, "Thank you, Ken. You've been a great help."

"Almost there," she said, and started scrolling through the contacts on her phone once more. She stopped and touched a listing, responding a second later. "This is Luciana Diez from Haven Home. You've just opened a file on a female child, last name Parish, P-A-R-I-S-H, first name Lulu. Can you tell me who's handling that case?" Pause. "Loretta Mills? May I speak with her, please?" Pause. "Now?" Luciana started to stand up, then sat back. "Two-thirty—in whose court? Womble? Thank you."

She buried her face in her hands. "We're too late," she said. "The court will hear her case and rule on placement . . ." she looked at the face of her phone, "in thirty minutes. We can't get there in time." She looked as if she would break into tears.

"We'll get there," Juniper said, pushing back from the table. "I'll get you there in time. Don't worry." He motioned to Ophelia, standing at the sink rinsing dishes. "Come on, Ophelia, we've got to go get Lulu."

"Let me get my purse," Luciana said. "I'll need my ID." She hurried toward the bedroom.

"Me too," Ophelia said, and started toward the stairway. "Maybe court will be running late. I hear that happens a lot."

Juniper stood at the top of the stairs, waiting on Luciana. When she ran back, he took her arm and although she was so upset she might not have noticed how quickly they gained the ground floor, they floated down the steps to meet Ophelia at her apartment. Going through the rental office they emerged onto the sidewalk. Neither woman noticed that the black Jaguar Juniper drove was no longer parked down the block, but was directly in front of them and he was urging them into it.

"How can we make it in time?" Luciana fretted. "Traffic is always terrible around the courthouse."

"Don't worry about it. Just leave it to me," Juniper said as he started the car. "I'll get you there." He heard a shout and glanced in the rearview mirror to see two men running wildly toward them. Doozy Collins' face was screwed into rage, and he was screaming obscenities as he pointed their direction.

"There she is!" he shouted. "There's the bitch who kept me in jail. She's the one who talked my wife into leaving me." He held something in his hand, and he drew it back in a throwing motion.

"I need to tell you something," Juniper said, facing the two women in his car. "What Lulu told you about me? She was right. I am a witch."

Chapter Forty-Four

■◆■

ONE SECOND THEY WERE sitting in Juniper's Jaguar on Old Main with Doozy Collins running up the street toward them, waving an unknown object in his hand and yelling obscenities at the top of his lungs. There was a flash, and the next second they were driving slowly on the street in front of the courthouse. Ophelia sucked in her breath and muttered something unintelligible, and Luciana gave a little squeak and held on to the door handle with her right hand, her left hand braced against the dashboard. A car parked directly in front of the entrance disappeared before their eyes, and Juniper slid his Jaguar smoothly into the space it left available.

"I didn't just see that," Ophelia said, putting one hand over her eyes and holding tightly to the seatbelt strap with the other. "I'm dreaming. I'm asleep and this is all a dream."

"Everyone okay?" Juniper asked. "Ready to take care of business?"

Luciana looked ashen, but she just nodded and opened her door before he could get out and do it for her. When he reached the passenger side of the vehicle, he opened the back door for Ophelia, who sat unmoving. "Ready to go see about Lulu?" he asked. She nodded and slid out, standing by the side of the car, shakily holding onto the side of the vehicle for support.

Juniper put one arm around Luciana and the other around Ophelia, and guided them into the imposing building. Stopping at the security checkpoint just inside the front door, the women put their purses on the conveyor belt, Juniper tossed the car keys on as well, and the three of them walked through the narrow opening one at a time. Had an alarm sounded, Juniper was ready to silence it with a blink of an eye. His hope to keep his magick power hidden was dwindling fast. The important objective at this point was finding Lulu, no matter what it took.

Luciana still looked a bit pale as she greeted the uniformed guard standing at the exit to the security post, hailing him as naturally as she could after being whisked from one side of town to the other in the flash of an eye. "Hey, Tom. How's it going?"

"Good afternoon, Miss Diez. Just fine. You?"

"Great, Tom," she said as she retrieved her purse. "Everything normal," she whispered, trying to reassure herself.

Ophelia, still mumbling under her breath, picked up her purse and Juniper his keys, and they continued along the echoing hallway.

"Judge Womble's courtroom is on the second floor," Luciana said. "The stairs are faster than the elevator." They swept up the wide, marble steps, walking rapidly until they reached the double doors with the number 210 posted on the wall next to them.

As they entered the courtroom, people were milling around, shuffling papers, greeting others, occupied in conversations, until a uniformed man with a gun on his belt took his place in front of the room, and everyone began to get settled. Luciana led the way to empty seats near the front just as the bailiff said,

"Quiet in the courtroom." At a nod from a woman standing near a door at the rear of the room, he announced, "All rise. The court is now in session, the Honorable Homer Womble presiding."

The man who entered and went up two steps to take his seat in a tall, plushy, leather-covered swivel chair, was a stout African-American man a few shades darker than the judge's bench behind which he sat. Both his deportment and his black robes gave prominence to his person. No way could an observer doubt who was in charge of these proceedings. The American flag and the state flag displayed behind him gave standing to the business transacted in this room.

As soon as the judge sat down, the bailiff said "You may be seated," and withdrew to the side of the room where he could observe everything that went on. Everyone sat except for a tall woman in a black business suit who remained standing behind the table positioned in the front of the room, and another woman who stood directly in front of the judge's bench, who spoke. "Case number 6530221. Matter of disposition of minor child Parish," she said and sat down at a small table directly to the left of the judge's bench.

"Your Honor," the woman in the black suit said, "Loretta Mills for the county, in the matter of the placement of the minor child."

The judge studied the papers in front of him, then looked over the top of his glasses at the standing woman.

"Why does the county have custody of the minor child?" he asked.

"Your Honor, the mother was arrested a few days ago in the . . . uh . . . police action . . . that occurred."

"The one that has kept our courts busy the last few days?"

"Yes, Your Honor."

"What was the charge?"

"Prostitution, Your Honor, along with other charges,

including gambling and drugs."

"And the mother has already been sentenced?"

"Yes, Your Honor."

"How long did she get?"

"Five to ten, Your Honor, with a minimum of four to be served."

"That long?" His eyebrows raised as he looked at Ms. Mills.

"Yes, Your Honor. She was on conditional release in another matter which was added back on when she was arrested again."

"Where's the father of this minor child?"

"The mother doesn't know who the father is," Ms. Mills replied.

"Doesn't know? Or won't tell?" the judge asked.

"Says she doesn't know. Says it was only one night, and she doesn't remember his name, even if he gave his real one."

"Hmm." The judge's eyebrows knit together as he studied the papers once again. "How old is the child?"

"She just turned ten, Your Honor."

"And there are no other relatives to take the child?"

"No, Your Honor. None."

"What is the county proposing to do with the child? By the way, is she present today?"

"Yes, Your Honor. She's in a conference room. I thought it was best if she didn't hear this part of the proceedings." Ms. Mills placed the papers she'd been holding on the table in front of her. "The normal thing to do would be place her in a foster home, but all the foster homes in the county are full, and this placement is going to be long term, due to the mother's sentence. The only thing left is a juvenile home, at least until a foster home opens up."

His voice rose as he said, "A juvenile detention center?"

Luciana popped out of her seat. "If Your Honor pleases, my name is Luciana Diez. May I offer myself as *amicus curiae*, friend of the court?"

There was a stir in the courtroom as conversations broke out on all sides at this unusual request. Judge Womble banged the gavel and the bailiff rose from his seat on the sidelines to say "Quiet! Quiet in the courtroom!"

"Miss Diez? It's been a while," the judge said in a friendly voice. "We've missed seeing you in court lately."

"Yes, Your Honor. I've been busy," Luciana responded.

"Seems like I've heard something about you being in hiding. Is that true?"

"Yes, Your Honor. It's true."

"Somebody trashed your apartment and is looking for you?"

"Yes, sir. That's true."

"So how did you get involved with this case? Is it all connected?"

"I know the child in question, Your Honor, but no, it's not connected with the reason I'm . . . er . . . in hiding, so to speak."

"You know the child? How? From another case?"

"She . . . uh . . . she frequents the neighborhood where I'm staying, Your Honor."

"What do you mean, Miss Diez, by 'frequents the neighborhood'?"

"Her mother would send her away from their living quarters when she was . . . occupied. I'm staying a few blocks away, and she would come to a nearby bookstore. I met her there and we developed a friendship."

"A bookstore, Miss Diez? You're hiding out in a bookstore?"

"Not exactly, Your Honor. The bookstore is close to where I'm staying, and she goes there to read."

"Goes there to read, hmm. I have questions about the reading material in a bookstore in the type neighborhood where a prostitute lives being appropriate for a child to read."

With that pronouncement, Ophelia stood. "Judge

Womble . . ." she started.

"Your Honor," Luciana whispered loudly.

"Judge Womble Your Honor," Ophelia added. "If I may?"

"Miss Jones?" the judge said, peering over his glasses at her. "You're involved with this as well?"

"Yes sir, Your Honor," she said. "I am."

"We've been missing you at church lately," the judge said.

"I've been missing attending, Your Honor," she replied.

"Are you in hiding as well?"

"Yes, Your Honor. I am."

"You are?" the judge leaned back in his seat. "I was being facetious when I asked that question. I've heard why Miss Diez is in hiding . . . word gets around . . . but what is your story?"

"The same folks as are looking for Miss Diez are looking for me, Your Honor."

The judge was silent as he stared at the two women before him. Finally, he shook his head. "Someone is after Miss Diez because she had him locked up for beating his wife, and he's after you because . . ."

"Because he thought I would lead him to Miss Diez. Then we thought he was going to snatch me and hold me until Miss Diez told him where his wife was," Ophelia explained.

"And all this led you to become involved with this Parish child?"

"Yes, Your Honor," the two women said together.

"And you're here because . . .?"

"I would like custody of her," Luciana said.

"Me too," Ophelia said.

"Ms. Mills," the judge said, "do you have any opinion on this?"

The tall, businesslike woman had been standing openmouthed, listening to the exchange. "Well, Your Honor . . ." She stumbled to a stop.

"I assume you're familiar with Miss Diez, who's a caseworker with Haven Home, and Miss Jones, who's the secretary there, are you not?"

"I've met Miss Diez, Your Honor, "and I've spoken with Miss Jones on many occasions. But . . ."

"But what?" the judge said. "You've already said that you don't have room for the child anywhere but in the juvenile detention facility."

"Neither of their homes have been vetted, Your Honor. And didn't they both say that they're living in hiding? Not even in their own homes?"

"That's true," the judge said, switching his attention back to Luciana and Ophelia.

"Where exactly, are you ladies living? And are you living together? We don't want to place the child where she'd have to be in hiding as well, or in danger."

Luciana's forehead wrinkled as she rolled the problem over in her head. If she revealed where she could be found, all their lives would be in danger. She looked at Juniper, seated between her and Ophelia.

"Your Honor, if I may speak," Juniper said, getting to his feet.

"Why not?" the judge said. "Seems like everybody else has something to say, why not you? Who are you, by the way? State your name for the court."

"My name is Juniper Penn, Your Honor." *Everything is blown to hell anyway. Might as well put the rest of it out there. I'll worry about fixing it when we get Lulu's business settled.* "I am a partner in Old Town Restoration."

"Is that who's doing all the work on Old Main Street?" the judge asked.

"Yes sir, that's us. Josh and Sabrina Pellegrino and myself are Old Town Restoration, and we're going to do even more than what you've seen already," Juniper said.

"What do you have to do with any of this?"

"That's where Miss Diez and Miss Jones are living, Your Honor," Juniper replied. "In nice apartments. Very suitable for a child, either one of them."

"I see," the judge said slowly. "And by extension, you're familiar with the child we're here to place."

"Yes, Your Honor. I know her as well, and I know either of these ladies could and would provide an excellent home for her."

"You know that, do you?" The judge once more looked over the top of his glasses.

"Yes, sir. I do," Juniper said forcefully.

"Without being too specific—giving away the exact location—I take it that they're both living in hiding somewhere within the ongoing restoration that's going on in Old Town."

"Yes, sir," all three of them said.

"Living together?" he asked.

"I have a separate apartment," Ophelia said.

"And you?" the judge asked Luciana.

"I live in a different apartment close to Miss Jones," she replied.

"Alone?" he asked, glancing back and forth between Lucy and Juniper.

"No, sir," she replied.

"Hmm." He swiveled away and stared at the far wall as he thought. "Ms. Mills," he finally said. "What are your thoughts on this?"

"Well, Your Honor, as I said, wherever we place the child would have to be vetted."

"Let us assume, Ms. Mills, that either home would pass inspection. And assume that I'd give permission for the child to be placed there temporarily, pending inspection by your department. Let us also assume that whatever we work out is better by far than putting her in juvie. Any other thoughts?"

"No, Your Honor." She paused, "except . . ."

"Except, Ms. Mills? Except what?"

"We make it a practice to not place a child in a home with an unwed couple. It would set a precedent if we did it in this case. It might lead to an unfortunate change in our practices."

"I could see that," the judge said. Looking at Luciana and Juniper, he asked, "And you two aren't married, are you?"

"No, Your Honor," Luciana said.

"Not yet," Juniper said, and Luciana and Ophelia both looked at him. He grinned back at them, at the same time wondering where that pronouncement had come from. It had just slipped out of his mouth without aforethought. But after it had, it felt good. It felt just right.

"Ms. Mills, I think it's time we had little Miss Parish join us," Judge Womble said.

Minutes later, the child who was escorted into the room was so unlike the girl they were used to, all three had to look twice. The black hair that had once shone in glorious ringlets was dull and nappy, not unlike dull brown cotton. Her skin that used to be a burnished gold was lusterless, and the eyes that had been filled with curiosity were now sad and lifeless.

"Louisa Louellen Parish," the judge began.

"Lulu," she said in a rebellious voice, "My name is Lulu."

Chapter Forty-Five

. ◆ .

"I KNEW YOU'D COME AND GET ME!" Lulu proclaimed for about the tenth time in as many minutes. "I just knew it."

Juniper eased his Jaguar in and out of the bumper-to-bumper traffic from the center of the city. He switched from one road to another as he headed toward Old Town. He could've blinked and transported the car to their destination, but he thought it might not be the wisest move. Both Ophelia and Luciana looked nervous as they exited the courthouse and climbed into the waiting vehicle, but they didn't mention the magickal trip across town they'd experienced earlier. Juniper wondered if they were going to simply ignore what had occurred earlier rather than deal with the proof that he was a witch. Lulu, clinging tightly to Ophelia's hand, got into the back seat beside her new guardian. She, however, hadn't been conveyed from one side of town to the other by magick, as had the two women, so she wasn't nervous at the possibility it could happen again.

"Those kids, the ones in that place—juvie—some of them were mean," she said as they pulled away from the curb.

"They'd hit me and shove me for no reason at all, and call me names. Not all of them. Some of them just cried all the time. I didn't cry." She paused and looked out the car window at the passing view. "I almost did," she said, and her quiet voice quivered. "But I didn't."

Ophelia squeezed Lulu's hand. "You're safe now," she said. "You're with us and you're safe."

"Yes," Luciana said. "We're here to protect you."

"When I didn't think you were going to come get me, that's when I was scared," she said, looking at Ophelia. "But I kept telling myself that you would. Mama always told me to have faith, that everything would work out the way it was supposed to. I tried to have faith, but it was hard sometimes. I tried to have faith that Mama would come back and get me, but the mean kids made fun of me. They said she was in jail and wasn't coming back, and that I was a baby for thinking that she would. I didn't believe them at first——not until the lady who was in court today told me it was true. She said Mama was going away to a big jail and wouldn't be back for a long time. She said she would find a new home for me, and that's when I started having faith that you would come find me." Lulu played with the hem of the tee-shirt she was wearing, twisting it in her fingers.

"As soon as we figured out what happened, we came to get you," Juniper said.

"For a couple of days we thought you were just staying home," Luciana said. "And then Juniper started asking all the shop owners if they'd seen you around."

"When they hadn't, I went to where you lived and the desk clerk told me what happened," Juniper said.

"That's when I started making phone calls and found out about court today," Luciana said.

Lulu snuggled up closer to Ophelia leaning her head against her arm. "I knew you'd come find me," she said again. "I kept telling myself you would, and you did." She closed her eyes. In a soft voice she said, "And now I'm safe." Ophelia eased her arm from underneath the sleeping child and wrapped it around her, pulling her close. She stayed like that until they reached the old neighborhood.

When Juniper rounded the corner, he slammed on the brakes before reaching yellow police tape that extended across the street. There were several police cars parked at angles, some blocking access to the shops, and two ambulances were nearby.

"What in the world has happened?" Ophelia mused.

"I'd like to know that too," Juniper said, knowing that he had spells protecting the property in every way he could think of, including the possibility of fire, even as he saw a fire truck parked halfway down the block and firemen dressed in protective clothing milling around it. People were standing around in groups, talking among themselves.

"Something bad has happened," Luciana said. "It looks like an explosion. The front of that empty building next to the rental office is gone and there are bricks and wood all over the place."

Juniper made a car at the curb disappear and he pulled into the now available space. "I'm going to go find out," he said, switching off the ignition and opening his door.

"Me too," Luciana said, opening the passenger door as well.

"Okay, but stay close to me," Juniper said, holding out his hand for her to grasp.

Lulu woke up when the car door slammed shut. "What's happened?" she asked.

"We don't know," Ophelia said. "Looks like something blew up."

"I hope it's not the bookstore," Lulu said, "or the teashop, or where you live, or . . ."

"I hope not too," Ophelia replied.

"Let's go see," Lulu started to open her door.

"Wait, Lulu," Ophelia said. "You stay with me."

As the four of them approached the crowd closest to the pile of rubble, a tall, regal woman broke away and drew near them. "Juniper! Luciana! You're safe. We were so concerned," Eleanor said, opening her arms wide to hug them. "And Lulu! We've been so worried about you." She bent and put her arms around the child.

Hearing the names, a policeman asked "Are you Juniper Penn?" as he walked up.

"Yes."

"People have been telling me that you're in charge of the property on this block."

"Yes, I am," Juniper said. "What happened here?"

"A man blew himself up, along with the front of this building," the policeman answered.

"Who?" Juniper asked, although he could've guessed the identity of the individual responsible. "Who was it? Do you know?"

"We haven't officially released the name, but we believe it was a man by the name of Doozy Collins."

"Why do you think it was him? Did someone identify him?"

"He had an accomplice who was walking—or running— along the sidewalk behind him. The accomplice fell down before the grenade went off. That's the only thing that saved his life. If he hadn't fallen, if he had been beside Collins, he would've been in little pieces like his buddy." The policeman glanced at Luciana, Ophelia, and Lulu. "Pardon me, ladies, for speaking so plainly. He's the one who said it was Doozy Collins. Did you know the man?"

"Not personally, but I knew who he was," Juniper said. "He'd been hanging around the neighborhood lately, threatening people."

"Threatening people? Anyone specifically?"

"Actually, officer," Luciana said, "he was looking for me. He thought I was hiding somewhere in the area—and I was."

"Who are you, and why was he looking for you?"

"My name is Luciana Diez. I'm with Haven Home, and why he was looking for me is a long story involving spousal abuse. I'd rather tell it in private instead of here where everyone can hear." She looked around at the crowd surrounding them.

"Aren't you the woman whose apartment was trashed a while back?" the officer asked.

"Yes, I am."

"I'm guessing that you didn't go back to there after that?"

"No, I didn't," Luciana answered. "It seemed necessary to stay out of sight with Doozy Collins looking for me."

"He was hell-bent on revenge," Juniper interjected. "In his mind, Miss Diez was responsible for his wife leaving him."

"That's what I gathered," the officer said. "Tell you what, you come down to police headquarters tomorrow morning so I can get the full story. There's still things to do here today to get the street open again." He looked around, then back at Juniper.

"You're the one in charge of the building?"

"Yes, I am. I'm a partner in Old Town Restorations."

"With the Pellegrinos, I understand?"

"Yes. That's right."

"Can you let me know tomorrow the extent of damage?"

"Yes, I ought to be able to do that," Juniper said. *You might have been amazed if I'd remembered to put a spell of protection on that particular shop even if it wasn't remodeled or being used. Oh well, I have things to do to it anyway, and it won't be any harder after this explosion than it would have been before.* "I'll come down to the police station with Miss Diez."

"Sounds good," the officer said.

"Would you look at that?" the policeman standing next to him said. "I've heard about tree huggers, but I've never seen one before."

Near to where the blast had occurred, a woman had her arms wrapped around a damaged tree. Her forehead was leaning against the raw wood, left exposed by a jagged slash in the bark. She appeared to be talking.

"Is she talking to that tree?" the policeman said.

Lulu's face lit up. "It's the tree lady," she said. "She's a h . . ."

"Horticulturist," Juniper interjected before Lulu could voice the term 'hedge witch'. *I'm going to have to talk to her about keeping some things secret.* "She's in charge of keeping our trees and plants alive and well."

"Horticulturist?" Lulu questioned. "That's what to call her?"

"Yes, it is," Juniper said as he shot a meaningful look at the child. "Horticulturists are people who know how to care for all kinds of plants. I imagine she's verbalizing what she's going to have to do to save the tree. Thinking out loud, so to speak."

"I'm going to go help her," Lulu said and ran toward the tree.

"And she does that by talking to them?" the officer asked.

"Whatever works," Juniper said and walked away.

Several people came up to tell him how glad they were he wasn't present when the explosion had occurred, as was feared at first.

"I was serving some folks seated on the patio," Alfreda said, "and they were sure they'd seen you right as everything blew up, but I knew you weren't in it." She patted Juniper on the arm and lowered her voice. "Got out just in time, didn't you? And the ladies with you?"

"Indeed I did, Alfreda. Indeed I did."

"Comes in handy, sometimes, our gifts."

"They do. Very handy."

"And you brought our girl back with you?"

"Yes, we did. Things will be better for her now. Ophelia was given custody of her."

"Really? That's good," Alfreda said. "Tell her she still has her job, if she wants it." She took a step away. "Got to get back to the shop. Business is brisk. Everybody wants to sit around and talk about what happened, and, of course, they need tea and cookies to have with the conversation. And coffee," she added. "I've added coffee to the menu," she called back as she walked away.

When he looked toward the tree again, the hedge witch was giving instruction on how to place arms around the injured maple. He walked over to them to find Lulu embracing the tree trunk, cheek against the bark and eyes closed. As he got close, he heard her soft voice encouraging the tree. "Please don't die. I've been away, and it was so bad that I cried sometimes, but I had faith that my friends would come and save me, and they did. Your friends will save you too. Have faith. The bad man is gone forever. Please live. Please live. Please live."

Chapter Forty-Six

■ ◆ ■

"THIS IS THE BEST FOOD I've ever had in my life," Lulu said. The adults at the table shot knowing glances at each other. The food her mother could have fed her while living in a cheap hotel room couldn't compare to the food on her plate now.

"That's what I like to hear," Harold said. "People what likes the food." He looked over the group. "Anyone need anything else?"

"Uncle Harold," Ophelia said, "tell Aunt Rose she's the best cook in town."

"I second that," Juniper added.

"I will. I'll tell her," Harold said. "She likes to hear compliments on her cooking." He went to the next table to check on the couple eating there.

"Can we eat here again sometime? Since I'll be living with you, and it's your aunt and uncle that run this place?" Lulu asked Ophelia.

"We sure can," Ophelia said. "Now that Lucy and I don't have to hide any longer we can eat wherever we want."

"Now that we don't have to hide," Luciana said, "I need to start looking for an apartment of my own." She stopped to take a sip of her tea. "And not in the same place I used to live. I'd remember everything he did to my home." She shivered. "I need someplace different."

Juniper stopped eating. The thought of Luciana leaving his apartment in Old Town felt like somebody had punched him in the stomach. "I thought you liked it living with me."

"I do. I like it very much, but it's your apartment. Your home." She looked at him intently. "I need a place that's mine."

"It can be yours too," he said.

"But I feel bad that I'm putting you out. I only endured it because I thought it wouldn't last—that you'd get your living space back as soon as we did something about Doozy."

"Endured?" Juniper repeated the one word that caught in his brain.

"I didn't mean it that way," she said. "You should know that I enjoy living there. It ought to be obvious that I do. But I'm uncomfortable putting you out."

"You aren't putting me out," he protested.

"Yes, I am," she said. "I've put you out of your bed."

"We could solve that very easily," Juniper said.

Luciana looked at the other people at the table. Ophelia and Lulu were watching and listening. "This isn't the time or place for this discussion," she said, and picked up her fork.

"Okay, we'll have it later, when we get home." He picked up his napkin, shook it, and put it back in his lap. "Our home." He picked up a roll and tore it in half. "Both of us."

Ophelia cleared her throat. "Maybe we need to talk about where I live, instead."

"Okay. Let's," Juniper said. He didn't sound happy.

"Seems to me I don't have to hide any longer either," Ophelia said.

"So you're going to move off and leave me too?" Juniper asked.

"Oh, please," Luciana said. "You're trying to make it sound like you're a poor little boy with nobody to play with. You're a grown-up living in a neighborhood full of friends and acquaintances. We aren't leaving you alone."

"Well, it feels like it." Juniper was surprised to find that it was very true. The thought of the neighborhood without Luciana and Ophelia in it wasn't as much fun, and since Ophelia was now Lulu's guardian, it would mean that the child would move aways as well. "I thought you were considering taking the job as our rental agent."

"I am. That is, I was. But now I have Lulu, and I'm in a one bedroom apartment. She needs her own room."

"I do?" Lulu popped into the conversation. "A room of my own? I've never had a room of my own."

"You must have forgotten who I am, or more accurately *what* I am," Juniper said. "And what I can do. A bedroom for Lulu can be done in a flash." He stopped talking before he inadvertently added "so there," to his statement, just like the child Luciana had accused him of being. He started eating again to keep himself from blurting out things that were better left unsaid, at least in public. Things like, "I'm a powerful witch, and I can do whatever I think I can. And I can magick a little girl's bedroom with no trouble at all."

All four of them were silent as they ate, thoughts and emotions tumbling around in their heads.

"Lucy?" Ophelia spoke.

"Yes?"

"Would you be upset if I take the job Juniper has offered me? The job of rental agent for the Old Town Restoration?"

"You mean, give up your job at Haven Home?" Luciana asked.

"Yes. That's what I mean." She pushed her almost empty place away and turned to look at her friend. "This is very interesting, this rental stuff I'm working on. I like working at Haven Home, but I like this too. "And this pays a lot better, plus not having to pay rent. I could save up money for extras, like trips or a new car or—she looked at Lulu—college for one or more people."

"One or more?" Juniper asked.

"I've taken a couple of business classes, and I've always thought I'd like to get my degree someday. With a loose work schedule, maybe I could do it."

"I think it's a wonderful idea," Luciana said. "It's the best thing you could do—for you."

"Then yes, Juniper. I'll be happy to accept the offer of the job of rental agent," Ophelia said.

Just then, Harold walked up to their table. "What you talkin' about bein' a rental agent?" he asked.

"It's my new job, Uncle. I'm going to be the person who takes care of renting the shops and apartments at the Restoration on Old Main."

"That right? Maybe you who I need to talk to?"

"How come?" Juniper asked. "You looking for a new place?"

"Looks like I'm gonna have to. My lease is about up and the landlord, he done told me the rent's goin' up."

"By much?"

"Yessir—a good bit. But the kicker is that he won't fix nothin'. The roof is leakin' out here," he said, pointing toward a stain on the ceiling, "and in the store room. He keeps havin' it patched, but it still leaks. If the health department comes by and sees it, they'll close me down. I just need a new place. The problem is, ever' place I look at is either too big or too small or costs too much."

"Uncle Harold, you come by to see me," Ophelia said. "I just betcha we can find you a spot somewhere that will suit you just fine, can't we Juniper?"

"Sure can, Harold. Give me a couple of days to get the debris from the explosion cleaned up, then Ophelia can show you what we have to offer."

After he walked away, Ophelia said, "Juniper, you're gonna have to help me get started with this."

"I will, Ophelia. I'll get you keys to the empty spots, and show you what we have. There's the end spot down the block from you, and we're about ready to start renting the properties across the street from us."

Minutes later, they piled into Juniper's Jag for the short trip to Old Main. If Juniper had been alone, he would have blinked and been home in one second, but he was afraid it would upset them to have another magickal experience so soon after the first one. He'd have to ease into performing magickal feats, and not hit them with too much too soon.

"I'll come by your place tomorrow and mag . . . er . . .make a bedroom for Lulu," he said as they all got out of the car.

"Oh boy," Lulu said. "Are you going to use magick? Can I watch?"

"Uh . . . maybe," Juniper said. "Go on with Ophelia now. You can sleep on the couch for one night, can't you?"

"Sure," she said. "But I usually sleep with my mother. I don't know if I can sleep alone or not. I haven't been sleeping very good since they took me away to that place. I've been having nightmares, and I wake up scared."

"Maybe you'd better sleep with me then," Ophelia said. "Until you get used to this new place."

Juniper followed Luciana up the stairs to his apartment.

"If I tell you I've been having nightmares and waking up scared, will you let me sleep with you?" he asked when they reached the top. He tweaked a lock of her hair.

"Would you be shocked if I tell you I've been expecting you to do just that for a while now?"

He reached out for her hand and pulled her closer to him. "Really? You mean I've been a gentleman for no good reason?"

"Being a gentleman? I thought you just weren't interested."

"Not interested? Hardly. I could barely keep my hands off you." He wrapped his arms around her, fitting his body to hers.

"You couldn't tell it by me," she said, turning her face up for his kiss.

"I didn't want to be too pushy," he said in between kisses. "After all, you were hiding from a dangerous individual. I didn't want you to think you had to do anything with me in order to have a safe place to stay."

"Juniper," she said, looping her arms around his neck, "I have money, I have smarts, I have whatever I need to take myself anywhere I wanted to go—a nice hotel, a luxury apartment— anywhere. I chose to stay because you were here."

"Really?" he asked and kissed her lightly.

"Really," she said and kissed him a little harder.

"Then let's go to bed." He caught her by the hand and led her down the hall to the bedroom. "I'll bet I don't have a single nightmare."

Epilogue

■ ◆ ■

JUNIPER WAS RIGHT. He didn't have a single nightmare, not that night or any of the nights that followed. Luciana went back to work at Haven Home, and often Juniper was called on to help when she had a case that needed a touch of magick to resolve.

He stayed busy in property development, as the Restoration in Old Town grew. Many new and quirky businesses opened in that part of town. Things you wouldn't think were possible could be found—if you knew where to look.

It took a few years, but Ophelia earned her degree in business and was eventually made partner in the company with Juniper and the Pellegrinos. Her savvy helped rebuild the old, forgotten parts of town. Although she gained confidence working around and with "special people", she never completely overcame being nervous when someone appeared or disappeared with a blink or the point of a finger.

Luciana and Juniper eventually moved to a larger apartment, but they continued to live in Old Town, where their many friends were.

Alf reconnected with his son, thanks to a TV weathergirl . . . er . . . weatherperson who could make it rain or snow at the drop of a hat, and they resolved the issues that had kept them at odds with each other.

The Haw treys remained steady and dependable. They never seemed to age. Trolls don't, you know. From time to time, the children and grandchildren and great-grandchildren would come to visit, causing shambles in the neighborhood, as rambunctious trolls are apt to do.

Alfreda's tea shop, the Cup and Leaf, became a happening place, with folk music groups playing on Saturday nights and poetry readings on Wednesday evenings. She furnished employment for many women and men that Luciana sent to her. She discovered a talent she hadn't known she possessed: she could see the gift that each person was blessed with, no matter how hidden or weird, and she poked, prodded and urged them until they used it, whether it was baking cookies, writing poetry, singing Celtic tunes, or predicting future events.

The Broken China shop and the Hutspeth's shop became very successful and people came from all over the state to buy their products.

And Lulu?

Lulu grew and bloomed. She visited her mother in prison every month. Ophelia took her and became good friends with several women who were there. She encouraged them to study to improve themselves, and several got their GED before they were released. One woman who was never going to be released earned her college degree and started writing books. Lulu's mother was well on her way to having a degree by the time she was released, and Luciana and Ophelia helped find her a respectable job. She rented an apartment in Old Town, and Lulu divided her time between her "two mothers", her birth mother and Ophelia.

And Lulu's gift? Her magickal talent? From her father? Who was he?

But that's another story.

About the Author

Nancy Smith Gibson has been a voracious reader from an early age, but didn't start writing until she had an empty nest—if you can call it empty when she shares it with a rescue dog and two rescue cats. She is the mother of four, grandmother of four, and great-grand of two.

Her professional years were spent as a "number please" and long distance telephone operator and supervisor, a census supervisor for various government surveys, and in real estate sales. For some years, she also produced crafts for sales at arts and crafts fairs. The people she met and situations she encountered provide rich fodder for stories.

She is also active in genealogy research, tracing her family roots back several generations.

She writes contemporary and historical 'sweet' romances, often including mystery and suspense, as well as magical realism and not-so-real witches.